Echoes of Old Souls

Echoes of Old Souls

by Nika Harper

Table of Contents

I.

The Song

Here and there, a song is played. In the very moment it is synchronous, falling upon the ears of many and the ears of special people who hear its call. The pattering drum beats are reflected in the fingers of new lovers as they find skin, inching up spines to soothe one another. The piano drips a rhythm overheard down an empty hallway as the glow of a forgotten stereo continues to breathe its melody quietly into a dark room, catching the attention of an eavesdropper who stops to think about nothing at all. The song travels along bowstrings to earphones in the street, a smile on a face, a night that was made better strictly by chance. The bass flows over lovers and the lonely, creeps through speakers and door jambs, shared by people who don't know they are sharing a moment.

Most of all, the song is heard.

It resonates a pattern that is felt and recognized without recognition, it makes people stop and notice. It's a visceral call to those who have had bodies, and who have felt the air between. All can hear this call, only few can answer.

It is played and speaks of memories so old they're unable to be placed. It speaks of times ahead and extreme change. It has a melody for hosts and their emotions over memories they'll never feel.

And it is just a song. Some don't even like it, no matter how it speaks to them.

For some, though, life is put on pause, and a new soundtrack begins. For four minutes, they have created a singular, standalone moment.

The song plays, and they remember who they were.
Then the song goes quiet.
And they remember who they are.

II.

Antoinette

ANTOINETTE WAS MORE FORLORN THAN OTHER PATIENTS, EVEN THE nurses could recognize that something was amiss. She was twenty nine years old, rather pretty in a plain way, and had clearly given up. The leukemia hit her later than most, but at her age she still should have had the youthful tenacity to fight it off-- were she to find a donor. Difficult, but not impossible, the doctors said.

Then why was she so sad?

It remained a mystery to the nurses, the orderlies, her visitors. A few of them figured a person knows when it's time for them. Sometimes they're just resigned.

This was different though.

Antoinette knew why she was sad. It terrified her to her very soul. Because she had a glimpse of what happened after death.

As she sat in her clean white bed, ignoring the window, ignoring the blank television and abandoned paperback books, she thought sadly that she might live through this, but she would be alone.

It's hard to keep secrets from yourself when you think them. It's easy to not realize something or not have it occur to you, but never simple to surprise yourself with planning. Her thoughts had been drifting for the past few months, and these were thoughts she had grown comfortable with, had come to rely on. It's why people knew her as who she was, and she liked that. She had these thoughts about leaving.

She was just left with the dread.

Annie was well liked, and seemed prettier than she really was. It was all in the decorum, her parents were proud and sometimes astonished that they had raised such a genteel young lady at times, if a bit worried about her. Her friends were kind individuals, not always intellectuals but certainly the type that preferred to share a glass of wine in a house than share a bottle of booze in a club. They would profess that she was a warm soul, polite and sometimes hard to get a read on. They shared her love of classical music, and occasionally they would cook her dinner as she told them about the beauty of timeless literature. These were not her friends since birth. Those people hardly spoke to her anymore. Annie had changed a lot since she was young.

In fact, a great change occurred while she was a teenager-- as high school often brings about in people. Her family was urged not to worry about it, these things happen, sometimes people just grow into who they are, all at once. One day Annie was just a fun little kid, popular with her school friends, maybe a bit irresponsible and air-headed, but to expect anything else of a high school student was silly. Annie was the type to go out to the football game. Then, almost overnight, she was the type that would stay in playing violin.

They didn't even know how she got the violin. Teenagers do funny things sometimes.

Only Annie knew what happened that year, as a senior in high school. To say that she knew was also giving her too much credit. They were passing by a museum one day, her and her friends, she remembered. She was holding a bag of new clothes in her hand, clothes she couldn't quite afford, and one of the posters outside spoke of new art exhibits including a beautiful streaky thing with reds, greens, colors she couldn't identify in patterns she didn't understand. It caught her eye for a second and she stopped to look at it, her curiosity getting the better of her.

Someone passed and spoke to her, quietly.

Then she had to sit down.

It was like she had been hit by an indefinable force, like a burst of hot air that she felt with her mind instead of her skin. She felt strange. The world felt strange. That painting was the strangest part. That was a silly thing to think about the art, because in that moment she remembered that her friend had painted it.

But did she *really* remember that?

Annie then excused herself from her friends, they thought little of it. She immediately returned the clothes before the store closed and bought a very different style. She laid in bed that night, her thoughts knotted and obscure, she wrestled with herself and her displeasure of the life around her. So it began to change.

Her group of friends transformed entirely. She stopped wearing trendy tank tops and designer jeans. It was like she was a new daughter, a new friend, a new person. Though disconcerted, her family loved it, and welcomed the addition of lace drapes to her room. She showed a mildly increased academic aptitude that put her through school at a local but solid university, studied literature and philosophy, wanted a job in a museum but got a job in a library.

Sometimes, her friends notice, you can see a glint of that previous, wilder, modern self. It hides in a wide, naive grin that is uncharacteristic. Then she will be serious again, her smile returned to its subtle and lovely state, the twinkle in her eye off traveling elsewhere.

Antoinette had recognized something very important. She was not alone. Now, for the first time in twelve years, she might be alone again.

All of the memories and the innate feelings, these changes in personality that came so naturally and breathed through her, she understood only a sliver of what her new life was and why it was that way. She sometimes spoke to herself before feeling aptly silly, but it truly felt as though she was not herself at all. There was a comfort in that. A passive decision making that she had grown to trust, a demeanor that she had taken to readily, but one that was not her own. She was aware of the disparity now, the dissection of person with personality, at a time when part of her was threatening to leave.

She had never felt crazy. Antoinette merely felt... nice. For twelve years, things went well. She shared her loves and grew to new ones. She absorbed minor talents and preferences. She enjoyed the polite attentions of men and sometimes pursued the attentions of women. She could taste the difference between regions of tea. She supported her dark-paneled life and knew which fork to use if the rare opportunity came up. People loved her for her mysteriously-acquired culture. She loved herself for it too. It was stepping into a new life that she never knew she wanted, and it let her breathe.

She was only twenty nine after all. She had so much more growing to do, there was always something to refine and she caught herself having doubts, thoughts about the time wasted on the endeavour, the reluctance to let a project go. She wasn't thinking about life and survival as she thought these things, she was thinking about it like a house you have built and must evacuate. It wasn't about ending. It was about loss of a resource. It was subtle too, but she felt it, and she began to be scared in the part of her she recognized to be her innate self. She woke up from autopilot to realize her support was leaving.

Stranger still, where would this support go?

The doctors were kind. What they said often made sense if she had been paying more attention, but her thoughts were split and distracted, even at these tense moments. By even getting sick, being sick, the chance of dying meant that as a person she was infirm. The foundation was rotted at a young age, the structure had come into question and faith was evaporating. Would it be better to move on? No, she pleaded, not sure what this meant to her future. Being young of mind, she responded unattractively by sulking. She had a lot to sulk for, and a lot to think about yet no private way to do it.

Antoinette had proof that her life may be ending. But she wondered, and had proof inside her, how permanent that end may be. The mysteries of continued existence were all the more daunting with the evidence she held. There were only more questions. She asked them in herself and things were strangely quiet, it would appear even she did not know the answers. The comfort she always had from a shared mind was lost, both sides were unsure of what to do next, the synergy had broken. All due to illness of a body that was joint property.

What would a pianist do without fingers? How would a mathematician survive if he lacked logic? Her dependence was comfortable for so long, nor was she mature enough to cope with the possible loss without fear.

Would she also stay in the world?

Did she have anything to offer, if she did?

She became a jealous lover, only making her seem more ugly. Antoinette began to fight herself again, wrestle her inner thoughts and fears as she was an increasingly less palatable vessel for whatever this movement was within her. She considered her failings. She ignored the beauty in others, for the envy in her own heart. The downward spiral continued and fed itself, left her sitting in a hospital bed again wondering what she could do to save her life in a way that had little to do with infected marrow.

The nurses noticed that she was fighting an emotional battle, and as a person without a child, husband or even a boyfriend to speak of, they could not fathom what inner turmoil this poor girl was going through. Her violin was dusty on the shelf next to the bed. They held her medical notes clasped in their hands, and she had a good chance of survival. Her displeasure was mysterious. If her life will continue, then what was she so occupied with losing?

They parted from the doorway and continued their rounds as a handsome young orderly brought in fresh pillows for the sleeping patient. Antoinette was quiet on the bed, stirring in the slightest to look at him with glazed eyes. She was pretty, he thought as he bent to adjust a pillow beside her, then he tripped and fell to his knees. Instead of being alarmed, the girl in the bed curled up tightly, squeezing her eyes shut in her sleep.

"Poor Annie," he whispered, and stood up straighter than before. He went to his manager's desk to call out sick for the day.

The room was left colder. Annie shivered in her bed, alone.

III.

Adam

THE GALLERY WAS BRIGHTLY LIT AND PACKED WITH PEOPLE, THE BUZZ of conversation carrying words about extravagant pieces set far from the main exhibit. The lopsided ceramic pot with living glaze was worthy of discussion for its strangeness. When approaching Adam's star piece, the onlookers became quiet and pensive, avoiding his stare.

The perfection of it made it uninteresting.

He deserved to be there. Adam had the patience of an angel and hands to match. The gallery tonight focused on modern, abstract pieces in his collection: the slope of female curves in deep, contrasting colors on black velvet. The pieces came alive in some very familiar way, though they were not realistic. The crowds murmured appraisal, some shifting their eyes elsewhere as they sipped their drink. The unspeakable intimacy with the subject was startling. It was mere brushstrokes, but it nearly breathed.

Despite the content of his art, Adam's preference remained indeterminate. He paid no mind to the romantic attentions of others, no matter how enticing the presentation. He was the untouchable artist, and it only added to his allure. His handsome, polite smile did not reach his eyes; very few words escaped his lips, even when pressed for comment. The crowd was empty to him. Full of people, so many black gowns and buttoned shirts and clinking glasses of wine, he'd seen the gamut for years back when galleries were cathedrals and he painted wings onto women on whom they didn't belong.

Was he ever great?

No.

Art was always an incredible talent of his, and in his youth, Adam had all the makings of a brilliant future. He enjoyed it once, painting all manner of things as much as he could, learning what makes a haystack translate to the canvas, and learning why haystacks were important enough to paint. He applied himself with ease and skill, to fanfare and great effect.

Then one day he drew a woman.

He continued to learn under the keenest minds and the gods of art until they would help him no longer. He learned a thousand different ways to paint, forever defining his inspiration that mentors called wasteful, as their frustrated fingers twitched for the talent in his. The years were not always kind to him, and others were too kind out of foolishness. He had lived in lavish lifestyles with canvas at every elbow and the finest cloth on hand, he had been offered palaces in exchange for his talent. He was fawned and doted upon, for reasons of love... but kindness does not always buy affection. Adam was not cold, but he was not appreciative. His heart was elsewhere.

Every single one of his pieces was the same woman.

He had tutored under those with names found in old museums, mimicking every art he came across with precision and taste, but he was rarely the one in the spotlight. He practiced and learned with vigor until he was an expert, but so rarely an innovator. He did not seek a fortune. He wanted to create. He wanted to create her.

Forever.

With each new skill, she breathed anew. Within hundreds of years she had been perfected, as though she stood with him in every room to pose differently, flawless in reality.

Others had loved her, for she truly existed to Adam and that breath of life was given to every new portrayal. His sensuous knowledge of her curves, and the slight, private smile she sometimes held was so enticing, it was easy to believe she lived among them. The paintings were sometimes collected by others who found them intriguing. Masterful. Excruciating. But none loved her as Adam did. Their souls went on, but Adam's stayed. He had work to do, and a woman he would dedicate a thousand lifetimes to, had he the chance.

He would lay in bed, transferring his bedroom to the canvas and painting her within it. He would paint her within his world as though she was using his bath towels, wet with the water from his home. Sipping the coffee from his mug. Sharing a Christmas morning together, quietly, as she unwrapped oranges and fine fabric dresses. She was ageless and so was her era, it changed by pure mood and style. Those close to him knew her name.

Verona.

The great, untouchable Adam. Hero to romantics who idled their days away on love and fancy. Enigma to the critics who wondered why his talent had not diversified. The great, untouchable Verona, whose curves made onlookers blush as though they were inches from her bare body, whose sheer lack of existence made one man an outcast though every artistic era in the world.

How could he love another, when he created her?

Verona danced alone in lavish dresses, on the backdrop of fine wood paneling and glossy floors. She read books alone on balconies where the sunlight served to accent her body and provide light on pages, and the view existed to show her to the world. She cooked alone, with copper pans well worn by years of her hands preparing carrots and herbs. She painted her fingernails with no makeup on, preparing for the next day. She plucked away at an instrument, sober and determined, her ear tipped to listen carefully as it was tuned. Oh Verona...

Verona could not exist, but Adam would continue until she did. The art of ages would precede her.

The lights came on. The dust had barely settled on his exhibits. His seat was right where it should be, outside the crowd. The drinks were passed about in hands, fingers met in introduction, another gallery night was upon them and Adam let his body language do the work. Admire, it said, but do not meet. It is not my work, it's hers.

His eyes were elsewhere, his attention fleeting, passing from perfected forms on diverse canvas to flimsy bodies in the audience. It was nothing of note. Black shoes. White business cards. Dark hair, framing an oval face. Adam slowly stood up, moving inches from this new figure in front of him, a woman whose eyes confidently and patiently locked on his. They were blue as bathwater, they were brown as a mahogany throne. They held memories: all the glossy floor dancing,

16

all the elegant hair pinning. He was looking into the eyes of Verona, yet nobody saw her but him.

His thumb reached out to brush the slope of her cheek and she smiled in warm relief. It was her smile, shining through. He wanted to touch every part of her, to check every last detail and discover more he hadn't seen. The soul was there, shining through to him. It was worth all the years of art, of supplies, of paint, of revisions and recapturing, of mediums new and old. Adam was gazing into his perfection, and he knew he would spend the rest of his lives dedicated to this same art. To the shape of her toes, to the smile in her sleep, to the twinkle of a tear on her cheek. He saw what was not there for anyone but himself.

Now his calling was different. He had to show what could not be shown. As though they had always known one another, and as though no words were needed, she put her hand lightly in his and they turned to look at the art he had made, as others admired it too.

They had forever. So they enjoyed the moment together.

IV.

Donovan

"WE HAVE A FEW YEARS, YET," GRANDPA SAID AS HE STIRRED THE spoon in his cocoa. He liked his with a bit of brandy in it— as is the privilege of his age. Don just liked his plain. At nine years old, it was hard to see why adults liked alcohol because to him it tasted so funky, so little Donnie just watched as Grandpa poured a smidgen of dark liquid into his cup with a wink.

Their fireside chats, as Grandpa called them, always stood out in Don's mind. He liked the peaceful parts of it, and he made Grandpa tell him stories about old America and cowboys and the West. He knew somehow that Grandpa wasn't old enough to have been there, but he spoke as though he could see every detail, so it was like listening to a movie instead of watching it. He wondered if that's what books were like, for right now they were mostly about solving mysteries or scary ghosts in the attic. Maybe other books were more like Grandpa's talks.

They'd been getting together like this for years, Grandma would nod at her husband and head upstairs to bed, and Grandpa would always address him by his full name for the entirety of the discussion. It would usually be at night, but not too late, and there would be a fire. There was never an introduction, there was just cocoa and Donnie learned that meant he would hear about the big world out there again. Sometimes he would get sleepy, or would get bored hearing about how people made little tents out of newspapers on the streets when everyone was poor a long time ago, but it sure beat reading it from a book like his teachers said. They should bring in Grandpa to teach class, Don would think, he makes stuff like war sound really exciting.

This talk seemed a little different though. Donnie was getting older, old enough that the stories were a little less cool than playing Playstation, and no longer at a point when pretending to be a cowboy was quite appropriate. It was a strange time for bonding, and Grandpa secretly knew that in a few years Donnie would be "too cool" to want to hang out with his grandparents in any respect.

Don saw the cocoa and settled down to what would be one of the strangest conversations of his life.

Grandpa sipped his cocoa carefully, surveying Donnie as they sat face to face. It was a cool night out, but the room was very warm with the flickering orange firelight, and Donnie liked the shadows it played across the furniture.

"So what do you like to do, Donovan? What are your hobbies?"

"I play games sometimes. I like to run. I like being outside in the grass, and playing tag. I like..." he wanted to say he liked girls but he wasn't sure if that was true, or just because he'd seen it on the TV a lot. "I like school and adventure and math."

"I also like all those things," Grandpa smiled, leaning back with satisfaction. "Mathematics is very interesting to include. Do you like science as well?"

"I dunno, like mixing chemicals and stuff? We don't do that."

"Not entirely. Science is like math, but applied to the world. Things like, how many stars there are in the sky, and why they exist up there, what they're made out of, how far the moon is away from us and why we only see one side of it. That's some science."

"I wonder about that stuff, yeah."

"We'll just have to see how well you do as you grow up." Grandpa sat back in his chair, pleased, "You seem to be a straightforward, logical thinker, and I appreciate that. I've been many things. I've often been a dreamer, and I'm not sure I liked it too much."

He got quieter, and started to speak slowly as Donnie leaned in to listen harder. "When I was a very young boy, I played with little trucks and cars in the water ditch out back of the house. There was no one there, just me. My sister was four years younger and was too small. The nearest neighbor was a quarter mile away, so I learned to play alone. My imagination filled in all the vacancies. I used to see some small lead metal soldiers at the local store. They were too expensive to buy so I just dreamed some more. I saw in a magazine how to make these little toys by melting lead and pouring it into some molds that were available, but also too expensive. So I dreamed some more.

His glasses caught the light from the fire and shielded his eyes from view in a reflection of rippling flames, "The old mind can really build a world of its own. Each generation comes along and has dreams, dreams just as vivid and real as any of my day. So today, the dreams are different."

Donnie watched the firelight glow in the lenses of Grandpa's spectacles, and thought briefly about what dreams in the future would be.

"I've been a child many times and dreamed the dreams of children," Grandpa continued, "I've written my real adventures down in private and lent them out to experts who value my insight. I've learned that being a child is too hard on an old mind, but sometimes there was no choice. I believe this country needs me as much as this family does. I think you'll understand what I mean someday. Do you like to dream?"

"I don't know."

"Do you like to write?"

"Not really. Carrie does."

"I think it's something you'll get used to with time," Grandpa removed his glasses to polish them on his sleeve. "Your sister is a bright girl. Make sure you learn from her."

"But she doesn't play football with me."

"She is a girl, she might not like that stuff. I heard she likes to run like you do."

"We play tag with the dog sometimes."

The glasses went on again, "Do you play fair?"

"I try to, but Brutus cheats."

"He's a dog, he may not understand the game being played after all."

Donnie shrugged, "Yeah he cheats a lot though, so I have to cheat with him a little."

"...How does one cheat playing tag?"

20

"Say that you didn't get tagged, I guess. Brutus sometimes tags when he's not it, and runs away even though he should be tagging. So I sometimes do too."

"Cheating at tag isn't a very wholesome practice."

"Nah, nobody really cares who's it unless they're slow."

Grandpa smirked in his seat, "I suppose they would consider me one of the slow ones." His hands shook a bit as they held the cocoa, and the skin was mottled with age spots. Donnie had never seen anything like it before, were those like little bruises?

"How old *are* you?" Donnie asked, his curiosity finally getting the better of him. "Dad said you were seventy-something. But... you say things... Is Dad wrong?"

"He is, in ways, correct. Right now I am seventy-eight. But I am also much more than that."

"How?"

"I found a way to live a long time. But it's a secret."

"Can you tell me?"

"I think so, Donovan. I think I can." Grandpa stopped again, looking into his own cup, "Did you need a refill?"

Donnie looked into his cup. It was half full, but rather cold. He hesitated, and looked at it some more before Grandpa gestured to give the cup over, filling it up with steamy cocoa. It felt warm in Donnie's hands and he smiled. Grandpa always made it extra chocolatey so it was rich and felt like a dessert rather than a drink. He took a long sip as Grandpa added a bit more brandy to his own.

"Let's just say I'm getting my affairs together in one way or another. A lot of people do, before they die. Only, I learned how to do mine a little differently." Grandpa didn't look so reminiscent this time, he was straight backed in his chair, so Don was pressured into seeming attentive as well. "There's always the normal stuff, like having a will. Do you know what a will is, Donovan?"

"There's a couple things I've heard. My friend's name is Will. Then there's like, when there's a will, there's a way," Donnie said.

"Yes, that seems about right. 'Will' means a force of power, a desire to do something. You've heard of willpower, it is a strength of constitution. A will, as I am describing, is named for that very thing. It is a document that says where all of my possessions go when I die.

In the case of my death, I *will* items to be given away in the right ways. Does this make sense?"

"Are you going to die soon?"

"Everyone does, for the most part," Grandpa said. "As I said, I think I have a while to go, but in my experience, I can sense when it is growing near. I am only in my seventies now, but I have been much, much older. I have written many wills to make sure our family is taken care of. That's what a will is about. See this house? If Grandma and I go away, what happens to it? The will is made so I can give it to you, or your dad."

"Do we have to live here?" Don asked.

"No, after that you get to do what you like with it. But that makes sure it's still kept within the family. Except a will is for everything: the chairs, the bank accounts, everything I have has to be divided up, sorted out, and put away. Like cleaning your room, except bigger."

"I hate cleaning my room."

"You are lucky you have so many toys that you must clean them up," Grandpa said sagely. "In my life, I have accumulated a lot of stuff too, so it becomes a problem with organization before I move on. However, the material things are pretty easy. I'm good at writing up a will by now." He took a sip of his chocolate, "But there's a big thing I care about very much that I want to pass on. I need to make sure it goes to the right place."

There was a pause, as Grandpa sat expectantly. Donnie was a little frustrated, looking across at his grandfather. He really didn't look older than what he imagined a seventy year old to be. But he took the bait.

"What is it?"

"Something very special," Grandpa said gently, "You enjoyed the stories we've had over the years, yes?"

Don nodded, "Yeah they're cool. Especially the ones with the West and California and the Indians and stuff."

"What I am giving away," Grandpa said, "is a way to keep those memories. It's a big responsibility, though. It comes with a lot of pressure to uphold the family. To care for them. Have you ever thought about your family?"

"Like, Mom?"

"Yes, Mom and Dad, and also some day when you might get married..."

"Ewwwww, that's weird!"

Grandpa smiled, "It may seem that way. Do you know what you want to be when you grow up?"

"I dunno," Donnie looked at his hands, "I think you talked about cattle and horses a lot. I kinda want to do that."

"You'd like to own a farm?"

"Yeah, maybe, I guess. With horses."

"Have you ever ridden a horse?"

Donnie bit his lip and screwed up his face. He didn't like how he felt wrong.

"It's nothing to be worried about, Donovan," Grandpa said, "Right now, your life is limitless with experiences you haven't had, so it's difficult for you to know what you like, and where you want to go. Being a rancher is still a good profession nowadays. I should take you to the farm I used to tend. Though I think it might be a strip mall now. In my whole life, I've been... many things..." He leaned back in his chair, looking at the ceiling to give it thought. His round glasses glinted in the firelight. "A courier, a rancher, an entrepreneur, a soldier, a revolutionary. A businessman, a journalist, a philanthropist..."

"What do those mean?"

Grandpa chuckled, "They're all very different jobs, over a long span of years. You've heard most of the stories. I've been very rich and not so rich. I've worked very hard and then eased up a bit. I've taken care of quite a few families. Can you guess how many?"

Donnie counted in his head, "Like people in the family? 'Cause we have 8."

"No, no. Groups of families. I've had a few, raised a few households and had many children, more than just the ones we have now." Donnie couldn't tell what he meant by that, did he have cousins or brothers or something that he didn't know about?

Grandpa carefully continued, "I can tell we're going to go through some very difficult times soon, times of change. But these things need to happen in order for our family to keep growing and doing well. Your mom and dad know a little bit about what makes our family so special, and soon it will be the responsibility of one of you kids. It's a lot to ask though, keeping these memories alive. It's why I'm talking to you, Donovan.

"We've been a very lucky family, and I think part of that comes with practice. I've held many jobs, lived through most of America's history.... in fact, all of it, as far back as calling ourselves the United States of America. I love our family as much as I love our country itself." Grandpa picked up the fireplace poker and gave a few prods to the logs, launching sparks outwards. "When you fight to earn something, it becomes that much more valuable for you. I have the memories of fighting, you see. I was there with the Minutemen and saw our country's birth. I saw the battles of American on American, of individual rights versus the common law. I saw the fight to stretch from sea to shining sea, staked a claim personally in that frontier, made right and wrong decisions along the way." He dropped the poker, his gaze catching on the flames. Donnie thought he looked tired, and he stayed quiet to hear more.

"I'm not prepared for the future, but I have to be willing to go forward and see it. I still don't understand my cell phone that well. The internet is strange and tells me about things I don't remember. I think I'm ready for a change of mind, before I get too old to be impressionable. I need to learn again. You learn quite a bit, don't you?"

"Yeah, I learn a lot from you."

"I mean other things. You know how to operate the TV better."

"Yeah, there's three remotes but you only need two."

"These are things I'm starting to get slower about." Grandpa chuckled, "How much history have you learned in school?"

"I dunno, stuff about Columbus and the Pilgrims and stuff," Don replied.

"....Hopefully you don't think those happened at the same time."

"It's hard to remember when, because it happened so long ago."

"I agree," Grandpa said thoughtfully, "I must definitely agree. That is why I write things down, sometimes. The age of information, as they call it now, has been very promising for my manuscripts. I should get someone else to transcribe them, if only they could read my damn writing."

"Is it cursive?"

"A very old cursive. Was never the neatest at it, either. How is your penmanship?"

"There's too many loops in cursive."

"Can the teachers read it?"

"Yeah when I don't put the loops in it. I like printing. I think everyone does."

"That's good enough. You have the ability to see things very clearly."

Donnie raised his eyebrows, "I do?"

"Yes," the elderly man's voice sounded warm and wise, "It is fortunate of you, you should cherish it. Youth happens so rarely. How do you feel about growing up?"

"It sounds cool, Mom wouldn't make me go to bed so early."

"What about other things, like responsibilities?"

"I have to walk Bruce."

"There's a lot more to being an adult than that."

"Like learning to drive?"

"In part. But so much more," Grandpa said, and paused. "I think you should just enjoy being a boy."

"I do, I think. I wish I knew what it was like, though. Like, what the difference was."

"A very fine point to make. Maybe someday I can help show you."

Grandpa leaned forward, "I'm telling you this to see if you can keep a secret. Someday it will be time for me to move on. I want to make sure that I can trust you with the responsibility of the household, no matter how old you may be. Do you think I can do that?"

The room felt small and warm, his grandfather looked impressive in the orange-tinted light.

"I hope so, Grandpa."

"Would you let me help you live a good life, and provide for our family?"

"I hope so."

"Then we are in agreement, for now," Grandpa concluded, and pondered the thought for a moment. "You should develop more of an interest in history, Donovan. Sometimes, history is all we have, and I like remembering all the good details."

"I'll try."

"Is it time for bed?"

"Maybe," Donnie said, his stifled yawn giving him away.

They got up together and walked down the hall, the fire left to burn down and cocoa cups forgotten until tomorrow.

V.

Mona

THE MONTHS SINCE AUSTIN'S DEATH HAD BEEN COMFORTING TO Mona, as she realized it was finally over. It was hard to lose someone so important in her life, and yet important for all the wrong reasons, it seemed. The divorce had been difficult and insubstantial, the restraining order nigh unusable and, to top it all off, she just wasn't feeling as she should have. Maybe it was her fault after all. Maybe the years of screaming and bruises were what she deserved.

Austin wasn't always that way. They were both young people, pretty handsome. They lived in the suburbs, found love and started a new life together with their nice lawn and small house, not too far from their parents. She kept down a desk job and he jumped from career to career, acquiring skills but growing antsy all too quickly and moving on.

Mona had always feared that would extend to his relationship with her, but it did not. About some things, Austin could be a real bulldog, and it became surprisingly clear that he had no intention of going anywhere.

They never had children, or at least hadn't yet, and they did their best as a couple that was taking it slow and being lavished in praise of their families. His job paid for the house and her job paid the bills. They kept their love burning low and warm. Then Mona started doing everything wrong.

The dinner was unsatisfactory. Not as good as her usual. She used the same recipes, even, and thought she had done everything exact. Didn't matter, something tasted sour. Maybe the ingredients had turned. She would go to bed feeling a bit morose, as his arm wrapped around her waist for a goodnight hug.

More and more often, her cooking just wasn't what it used to be, just wasn't the best. He blamed the dish detergent, a broken refrigerator, or anything at all, but after a while he was partly fixing his own dinner. Then going out to get dinner before he returned home. Mona stopped mentioning it. She also stopped cooking.

Her clothing didn't fit quite right anymore. She only noticed it after Austin said something. She was getting older and her body was settling into new shapes, but she didn't know it would be so noticeable. He told her that white was no longer a flattering color. He told her that she should avoid sleeveless tops. He said the big belts brought attention to the wrong things. He wondered if she cared about herself anymore.

She had begun not to.

It was hard to tell on the timeline where it got bad. Maybe when Austin got home late and demanded dinner, but Mona was unprepared. He broke the dishes. Left the house. Came back just in time to say goodnight. She was confused and quiet about it. Until it kept happening. The dinners were not ready when he wanted them. What did she do all day? The laundry was not folded, it was just a matter of respect. He disconnected the phone because she was clearly socializing too much to keep their life in order. She reconnected it the next day, but he didn't mention it. The drinking began around this time. In retrospect, she was shocked that it had not existed before, and wondered if she just wished he had the habit so she could blame the booze and not him.

Bruises started appearing. It was never too rough, just in the heat of an argument, he would pull on her arm, or shake her shoulder. She began to call her mother, worried, and soothing words would get her through the night with promises of interventions and alcohol abuse centers. Alcohol was a drug that changed people, she was told, and things could be changed back. Are the finances okay? Are you okay?

Alcohol changes behaviors and not the person, but she was happy for the excuse, no matter how flimsy. She slept a little better, in her bed that might not have Austin in it yet, and considered what it would take to bring him back from the bottle.

28

It was all her fault. He didn't feel valued at home. She wasn't putting in any of the effort. She was just talk talk talking all day instead of keeping this household alive. She quietly agreed, she would pledge to do better, and when in turn she asked what he would do to improve, he slapped her. He said it was her problem. He said he loved her and hated to see her waste herself. Then he left the house again.

As he crawled into bed, arm closing around her waist, later in the evening than is appropriate, he said he wouldn't give up on her.

It was all her fault. She bought more powder to cover up the purple smudges around her eye, and wore dark makeup which suited her well. She was slimmer and her clothes became unflattering in their bagginess, but outside she looked almost glamorous. Her coworkers thought she was trying something new, maybe trying for a foxy vibe, and she passed off their compliments with a polite smile.

Her mother said she could start staying at their house, but... she didn't want to go backwards in life, to backtrack to living with her parents again. Look how far she had come! Austin just needed an intervention. It was that time in the week to try and discuss his problem, and to buy more makeup to hide the abrasions.

Mona watched her heirloom crystal shatter, and deliberately gathered each piece to throw in the trash. She watched their fights grow frequent. She felt the arm around her waist tighten each night, warm reassurance more like a cold shackle. She loved Austin, she wanted this to work. The breaking point was when she noticed she was bleeding. She cried, head hung low, in the corner of the kitchen and a perfect sanguine drop splattered onto the tile between her knees. She reached to her face, gathered a few days' worth of clothes, and stayed with her parents for the night. She didn't receive a phone call about it. She went to work the next day as though nothing had happened. The next night her mother helped her call up domestic counseling appointments and determined that the relationship was over.

But flowers showed up at her desk. They were lovely, roses and baby's breath just like their wedding bouquet, and there was no tag but she knew it was from him. Without telling her mother, she went home that night, and prepared a dinner that went cold as she waited.

He said that makeup made her look loose.

He said she should stop trying to look like a hooker so the boys in the office would look at her.

He said her dinner was cold and terrible.

Her arm was so bruised it was numb. She got more clothing, more supplies, filled up the car with what she could and went to her parents' house. They wanted to call the police. She wanted to call a lawyer.

The phone calls started, the harassment began, and Mona was not immune to it. She listened to every message, changed her number and watched as the messages piled up there too. She split the joint accounts, she sent the papers over and she hid from her social life. Her friends were getting the same treatment. Restraining orders were filed, but he was just another abusive drunk among the mix. Her father had a shotgun and it sat by the door, for how many times Austin came knocking and refused to leave.

Mona was stuck.

Then it all changed. A call reached her parent's home, and she answered to hear from the hospital, that Austin had been in an accident and he did not make it.

Somehow this made it all worse.

They would never be in love again. He would never be who he really was. There was no chance of redemption, or salvaging the life they had worked so hard for. Everyone said she was focusing on the wrong things, that the problems were at last over, but she couldn't help but mourn the man she continued to love, under all that had gone wrong.

The phone calls were done. The house was sold and her new apartment was clean, but lonely. She got a cat and gave it away. She signed up on dating sites and discontinued them. It was too early to start her new life, so she continued on as best she could, not trusting others because of her loss of love, and her betrayal of abuse. But slowly things began to change, where she thought about going by her full name, Magnolia, or a nickname like Maggie. She bought some new clothes without the residue of criticism from her dead ex, and after a year and a half... she found someone nice, and new.

Richard, the guy everyone wished they had. Sure they worked together, in different departments, but it shouldn't affect their life at all. A little office romance is just what she needed. He was patient, adoring, and after a few months she started cooking him the occasional dinner, with much apprehension. They became a beautiful adult couple, he would take her to Napa on weekends just to wine and dine her, and she would share couch space with him as she puzzled on crosswords. It was the right amount of comfort for a pair of divorcees.

A weekend trip with his parents caused some stir as they claimed how lovely the two of them were together, and how Richard had changed into a different sort of gentleman. He was always polite, they said, but now he seemed so edgy. They liked that she brought out the hip side of him, and he smiled and put his arm around her waist. His thumb caught on the belt and he flinched, leaning in to joke about how he didn't like that belt much. And she froze. But the night moved on.

Her dinners were still occasional and good, as she experimented with new recipes and new kitchen sets. Mona enjoyed cooking and the feeling of placing a warm meal in front of a good-looking man. They sampled their dinners, and that night, something was a little off. He said it wasn't as good as had been before. And she froze. The dinner went on.

They cleaned the dishes together and he sensed a discomfort, which they quietly discussed. She was hurt about his comment, but he didn't apologize. He defended it and said he didn't want to lie to her, and as she turned to leave the kitchen he grabbed her arm to get her to listen. And she froze. And she stepped away. And she asked Richard to leave.

Everything was good and normal again in a few days, and so stupid of her to cause a fuss about it. Little Maggie, she'd think to herself, with her head all scrambled. Richard was just being honest, and they made their amends and made their dinners, and made their life whole again. It had been many months of being a pair, him calling her Maggie like everyone else had started to do. They said it suited her better and she agreed, so she was Maggie in this new life, trying to distance herself from the blocks of the last problem, which was gone. The completeness of her previous relationship was unparalleled, he could hurt her no longer. Of course, a silly statement could bring that up again once more.

She even decided to wear that belt again, she thought an over-sized accessory made her look good, but Richard had that look... He shrugged and said, it didn't bring attention to the right areas. She took it off and threw it away. A belt was not worth her sanity.

Richard would stay over and they had found their positions in bed, slightly changing their posture to fit another, and his arm would wrap around her waist. She would remember. And Richard would say, reassuringly, that he wasn't going to give up on her. She didn't sleep well that night.

She didn't call her mother. It was just silly things left over in her head, and it put a new light on how hurtful her relationship with Austin had been. She was starting a new relationship with old scars. She was sure Richard had them too. She made him dinner proudly. Then he wondered if one of the ingredients had spoiled.

The arm around her waist felt tighter that night.

She couldn't have this happen. She brought Richard over to tell him they should take a break. Things were getting to her and she needed space. She was confused and still dealing with the past. Instead of being hurt, he seemed angry. Maggie tried reasoning and saying it might not be long, maybe she could just take a vacation alone and get her head right. They stood close and talked, but he was adamant she should not leave, and when he grabbed her shoulder and shook, she stepped away and said it was over entirely. They were done.

The blood on the tile floor was a shock as she watched her nose dripping, splattering in patterns on the ground between her knees. He kneeled down to face her and through watery eyes she looked out at him, out at a man who was not Richard and could not have been for a while.

He told her he wouldn't give up on her, no matter what a tramp she had become and how little she cared about him. He had hope that they could work. He was not going anywhere.

Mona didn't move as Richard left the apartment. She didn't even reach for her phone. Startled and staring at the blood on the tile, she knew what those words meant, and how they were said. She would never be left alone.

Her phone started ringing, and the messages came in, how he wouldn't give up on her, how they deserved another chance and he would make sure she never forgot how good he was to her. He said they could get the old house back, and that Richard wasn't really necessary, he could be anyone, and he would be. They had made a promise and a vow. In this time of her failure and suffering, he was not going anywhere.

She listened to every message.

VI.

THERE WAS A STORY THAT WENT AROUND WITH THE GIRLS IN THE industry, and they were superstitious enough to believe it. In their line of work, they had to be. Any moment was a big break, any tiny detail was important. Hardly anyone knew about the phenomenon, but between the girls it was spoken with reverence and whispers as they peered around for the next hint of truth. Everyone was suspect to the jealousy of wanting to be good enough. All models are superstars. Some are just worth more than others.

It was hard to tell what was characteristic about it. Was it the smile? The twinkle in her eye? What really made her who she was, and how could you identify it? It really was just that certain something, "the sauce," the *je ne sais quoi* that made fame what it was. With careful eyes, the eyes of the envious, you could see the power influence others. There was no way of telling for certain.

The whispers and tales told of a power, as though some kind of talisman or trick, that changed people into stars. It was as though they were empowered with fame itself, they become beauty incarnate. Some of the sillier girls, the ones pretty enough to not need to think, believed it was material. They would become religious perhaps, or feed into spirituality with mentors. They would pose, with lockets clasped in their hands, eyes on the camera, head filled with mantras. Whether they made it far was of no consequence. They did not have this power. Some claimed to have been overcome with it, in the same way allergies can be cured by placebos. It did not bless them, and the world knew it by the fact that the world did not know them at all.

34

The more intelligent ones or the more informed, knew that you could not look for it. It was given, or it was not, and there was only one of it, eternal. Through the hive mind of many models over many years, little hints had been discovered and tracked. It was so clear, seeing the cycles of models whose names were golden, who stayed in legend and that golden age never overlapped. They may stay famous, sure, but something had changed, and a new starlet had risen to worldwide acclaim.

It was also felt by those around the gifted girl. A model may be wonderful one day, sure to be famous without any help but not quite there yet, and as she digs around in her makeup bag she talks with the other girls as though they are all friends.

One day that might change, and the situation becomes palpable. She might become more reserved, but suddenly, without trying, the air around her feels different. Her hair sets just right, and even in a shot with five other women, the camera is always focused on her. She becomes the centerpiece, so magnetic even the other women cannot help but look on. Suddenly she is a woman of awe, and it is hard to believe that once, those girls spent any time with her at all.

Was it truly the smile? The look? The eyes with their practiced magnetism? The body that eased into all the correct positions, as though it was made to do nothing else? A woman became an icon, a photo editor became a disciple and a magazine became an altar.

There she was again.

This power, they called it Her, they called it She, and it must have existed for a long time but the actual date was a mystery. The earliest stories with any credibility were in the early 1900s, back when cameras were still new technology. Before then, it could have been anything creating these stars, if many existed at all. By the advent of photos and visual worship, she was definitely a presence. She sometimes was in cigarette ads, or a film or two, her eyes smoky with the haze of mystery and allure. The world became art when she was in it. Desire was made visible. Then she would move on.

She had no name. It had been too long since she used it. It was impressive, a person so successful, ceaselessly at the top of her game and the driving force behind beauty. Every time she was met, she was a different type of beautiful. Always a different shape, style, woman. Yet still ultimately and indescribably herself.

She had as much style as anyone could ask, never sticking to one culture or type, and she expanded to the role more artfully than a method actor. She was centered and businesslike, a dream to work with and a role model to professionals: she was the perfect canvas. Her lipstick never smeared. Her clothing was never a burden. There was a delicate sweetness to her demeanor, like spun sugar under every bobby pin and layer of powder. She made the right decisions. She made everyone else look better. Yet in some way, she wasn't real or touchable. She walked among the rest and they felt blessed, but never comfortable.

She had been everything, and the success was hard to track. There she was, elegant in petticoats where blinking would blur the photograph. A cigarette clasped in manicured fingers, smoke curling into the perfect frame of a face and mirroring tightly wound hair, she would gaze with the same wanton eyes as she had when she created the art. She was a burlesque queen, wore tattoos like royal finery, posing in polka dot heels with pursed lips, making them all think, damn, now that's what I call a woman.

She created queens out of ladies, dictating the life of each paragon in the works, gaining respect no matter the medium. Scandal was impossible, no matter the tumultuous culture in which she found herself. It was difficult to gain her favor, in all her changing forms, but some could. Prestigious photographers, brilliant business owners, keen-eyed folk who didn't gossip would quietly sense when she had returned, and her patronage would benefit all involved. Occasionally they would bask in her presence, ask her how things had been, and she would respond with a pure smile that would not meet her borrowed eyes. Mysteries to one another, they might be, but a pinnacle to all those mysteries, was her. She was good business, good press, good people. The shallower models saw this trend, these places, and haunted there as they could. It's too bad, the places were already haunted.

How many women had she sailed to stardom? Fifty? Even more? Was she the key to their success, or was she preying on their talent to live in the spotlight again? Nobody dared ask about her. She was an ascetic. To be in her presence was satisfaction and trust, and none would dishonor by asking too many questions, even after she had moved on.

...And there was always a time when she would go. Sometimes these new stars would fade into obscurity, but most had learned the ways and were able to continue their lives with the right poses, the perfect stance, the posture, the smile. They would let themselves shine through. They would develop their own art and character. They would lack the glow she gave. The golden age was ended, but established success kept on.

She brought a certain something to the world. A power, a charge, a magic. It was turning greatness to perfection, beauty into crystal, loveliness into a life form. Perhaps she was Aphrodite. She was the closest thing anyone could know of it. Admirers would think, I may not believe in God, but now I believe in God's creatures, and the beauty of all things. She had ascended.

My, how the girls wanted her. How they would curl their hair just right and hope that they were the next to be so special, to be in the eyes of whatever power this mystery was. How they followed their superstitions somewhat stupidly, and clutched their spirituality books and painted themselves with fragrant oils to harness the inner goddess. They put on their clothing, tight. They placed their bodies carefully, posed. They closed their eyes and waited, hopeful that they would be found. Inevitably, those of pure beauty would pay no mind, until without knowing nor asking, they had become another woman entirely. Until they had the tutor of a lifetime, and many lifetimes before, and they ascended to the stars.

VII.

Laura

THE FERRY WAS PULLING UP TO THE DOCK, COMMUTERS CHARGING
ahead toward bridge exits, and into a chilly day in Marin County.
Laura wanted a drink. The pavement was wet outside and her open
toed heels were no match for the elements. It was only noon, but in a
vague way, she had an idea, a plan for why she was there.

Check that off the list: Boats. The ferry ride was tame and dull,
but she supposed a fear of naval travel would have outed itself on this
trip, if she had any anxiety. The checklist was getting longer, con-
tinually growing things she hadn't done and likely fears that she had
not yet tested nor conquered. It had contained many things: singing,
the dark, snakes. She even had a snake named Carl, just to prove it.
Newly checked off was boats.

...Did the fear even exist?

The world was so boring nowadays.

She wasn't the most attractive person, but she also had enough
money to sculpt her body however she pleased, and a few tucks in the
right places had meant her silhouette was a pleasant sight. It had been
an odd change, waking up in a new life without knowing how or why,
and finally coming to terms that she was no longer Laura, and that
whomever she was... was pissed. For years she existed comfortably in
that life, doing whatever her host did, but Laura didn't feel like doing
the nine-to-five anymore. Luckily, this new Laura had a rich family
who showed affection in large monthly allowances as a substitute for
any real family bond. It opened up a life of whatever she wanted, but
Laura had yet to discover what that was.

So far, no luck, and too much opportunity to keep trying. What was left to try? The ideas constantly weighed on her, sandwiching between other idle thoughts. What thrills were still out there?

Driving? She had bought an expensive car, and picked up a hotshot boyfriend to drive it fast.

Dentist? Her teeth were flawless. The dentist was cute. Whatever.

Maybe she wanted to dye her hair pink again. Maybe she wanted a friend. She was just bored.

It was hard to find a good bar in Larkspur, where all the alcohol seemed to be imprisoned behind tall countertops in restaurants. Of course, it being noon didn't help either. She doubted she'd get anything useful out of a typical mall restaurant bar crowd, if there even was considered such a thing. Mall restaurant regulars. The world is full of little agonies.

Was everything in the North Bay this drab? The patrons looked like farmers, not the affluent vacationers she was promised. She stood out in her classy coat, asking for their best wine and getting a glass of White Zinfandel. It made her smile. Through sparse conversation with the jobless dive bar patrons, she learned about a nice hotel in Sausalito, a shooting range further inland, and that Marin County had a soft spot for women with well-preened hair.

This plan seemed promising after all. She was on her way.

Claustrophobia? She'd gone spelunking in Florida, and the bats didn't make her nervous either.

Drowning? Scuba diving had no effect. Swimming classes, long trips to the beach.

Flying? In first class, nothing can faze you.

A few weeks of this, a few weeks of that.

Laura spent her mornings at the shooting range, and her afternoons gazing at the lackluster paradise that attracted people with money. Boring. She idly thought of reading books or exploring, but neither held her interest or was worth it in the end. What else was there to see? Should she buy out a gallery? Drag and destroy the displays of a china shop?

The Unknown? She'd taken trips to foreign places, without the help of language or familiarity. One city was just another city, each deprived farm town felt the same.

Death? Two months as a mortician. Besides, she had seen the other end of that already. Conquered that without even trying.

Laura was getting better at shooting and the attendants were getting a kick out of a self-assured woman in heels blasting away targets every day. One man caught her attention, or at least, his badge did. Officer Kellar. Thomas, to be precise. He was polite and helpful, with that slight hint of interest that accompanies all actions that go beyond the call of duty. He showed her disabling shots, recommended some less lethal guns and laughed when she said she wanted more. Then she asked for good places a girl could get dinner, though she'd rather not go alone.

He called her Ella, and he would bring flowers for her hotel room. She paid for dinner sometimes. It was polite and lovely, and it was driving him a little crazy, she could tell. She stayed distant and untouchable. But his badge was interesting, so she kept him around.

Commitment? Got married.

Loneliness? Divorced the sucker.

Sexuality? Hell, she even made money on this one.

So many check boxes.

Then Laura made her first visit to the Sausalito bank. It seemed nice, with expensive purses and bulging billfolds perpetually entering and exiting the building. She asked the teller if there was a safe for valuables she might be acquiring. Yes, they replied, would you like to see it?

No.

All in due time.

Authority?

Breaking the law?

...Interesting.

She bought a tiny little pistol at Thomas' suggestion, which fit snugly into her purse. It was cute. Then she went back and ordered a magnum. The attendant agreed with her, it feels good to have a nice fast car, even if you can't drive it like it *should* be driven. The gun was damn near illegal. Soon it would be very illegal. It was just for kicks.

Heights? Skydiving. Rock climbing.

Natural disasters? Rode along with tornado chasers.

The streets were quiet that evening, the sun making its last pleas across the sky, clinging to the walls of the bank with reluctance to let go. Thomas was going to meet her at the restaurant across the street around seven o'clock. Laura looked good that night, in a dress she had just bought for more money than it deserved, but it suited her. The taxi waited outside for her return, where the cabbie was annoyed but hopeful that Laura's expensive dress meant a large tip.

The bank was nearly empty, a few blue-hairs getting their finances in order with the reassurance of a teller instead of an ATM. She strode up to the counter, her heels were just the right type to click against the marble floor and catch the attention of the teller. He snapped on a smile, the type to help the rich people with their rich people problems, the smile of someone whose hands and eyes watched transactions their own account would never be privy to. There was an air of good service, and envy.

She had something she'd like put in the safe, this time.

That would be easy. Well, the manager has stepped out, but it can still be done, come with me.

Sex in public? Puh-lease.

Being poor? That was almost an interesting week.

The vault was lined with tiny safes, and she could have her pick. It was probably unwise to let a client back there but the teller didn't seem to mind, until there was a very large gun involved.

She wanted something. Anything will do. Open the safes until you find something interesting, then she'll have that.

Without any argument, he did. With a few fumbling minutes and jittery punched codes, a few safes were open and, glory be, there were some treasures inside. What a display of jewelry and gold. She decided she wanted it. It was all very quiet. Easy.

She could feel her pulse racing, just a bit.

What would she do with it? Who knows. Put it in the tank with Carl the snake. Prove she did.

Spiders? Tarantulas, black widows, biology labs.

Sharks? Cancun. Seven months ago.

Wolves? Camping in Alaska.

Her clutch purse carried newfound gems with little personal value, but Laura found herself satisfied. She walked out, her heels clicking against the floor, her gun proudly posed in front of her. The tellers all had their hands and eyebrows raised, somehow they had known something was up. She marched right out of the swinging doors.

Stage fright? Auditioned for musicals, movies.

Injury? Roller derby. No pads.

Dishonor? She'd need some in order to lose it.

Laura paid no mind to the flashing lights, nor the movement or yells around her. Her arm was sprained as it twisted behind her and she was slammed against a car, the yells of a cab driver claiming his innocence, a crowd of people watched. Her expression never changed as she was stood upright, lovely in her increasingly crumpled dress, being patted down by the rough hands of the law.

She looked up to see Thomas, well-dressed, at the entrance of the restaurant across the street, his face blank. She didn't smile, but she liked that disbelieving expression he had, she would take that with her. That poor fellow. He was stuck in his life and now alone in it again. She refused to be stuck anywhere.

Bound by metal links and shoved into the back to a police car, she went with a grace that made people uneasy. It didn't matter anyway. There was always bail, appeals, lawyers, pleas. In the very least, Laura was not stuck where she was. There was always a way out for her.

Besides. That was one less fear.

VIII.

Tanner

TANNER DIDN'T BELIEVE IN GHOSTS. THAT WAS PISH POSH, POPPYCOCK and all manner of demeaning names for silly superstition. He was un-affected by ghost stories told around campfires, spooky movies didn't bother him and supernatural documentaries were not in the least bit convincing. He always laughed at teased his friends for being afraid of such things, even when they were kids and would imagine them-selves to be Ghostbusters. They would make him pretend to be Slimer, because he was such a buzzkill. He was captured a lot. Such is the life of an aggressive realist.

Tanner liked science and explaining things. Mysteries weren't fun, solutions were. He worked hard to see that all questions had answers. In truth, it was sometimes insufferable. He was astoundingly good at trivia and the first to end a debate early by looking up the answer rather than puzzling it out.

He especially didn't like living in a place where there *were ghosts*. Come on, he thought as he heard these spooky stories, we should be beyond this, as people. He understood Halloween and the fun around it, but he didn't understand how a day-to-day paranormal occurrence could be taken as fact, the way many in his town thought.

Darla, sweet Darla, was a pretty girl, a decent intellectual, a college student who took classes on philosophy and wanted to be a school teacher. She wasn't a rocket scientist but she could talk about books and she wore nice stockings. Tanner had been dating her for four months, and they were *good* months. She had a warm heart and cooked warm meals. He liked how docile and domestic she was, a good realistic person in the world.

...Until she started talking about ghosts. She grew up with superstition; apparently, her mother had told her the stories and she believed it. They all did, in that town. It drove Tanner up a wall. Somehow superstitions get passed on and then infect the minds of those he actually might respect otherwise. It bothered him deeply that Darla, with the stockings and the sweet voice, could actually subscribe to such a thing. She had stories to tell, passed on from long ago through her family, and they had convinced her as well as any propaganda would. He felt his enthusiasm for the relationship fading. As Tanner grew into his late twenties, the pressure of this ghost-obsessed world pained him more and more, until one year he decided to prove it wrong.

There is no way to track supernatural beings, or at least nothing reputable that isn't a mistaken account of changes in air pressure, or faulty video recordings. He trusted technology to break in ways that were not mysterious, much more than he trusted the average human's ability to identify the true source of the problem. Ghosties were often to blame for problems that were primarily technical malfunction. Clearly, all he needed was to get a haunted camcorder with a bad battery. Finding the ghosts this way would not be sufficient.

There were haunted houses on every block, some would say. Old Indians in attics, mysterious laughter and occurrences all around the place. In any older city, these things were bound to happen, and be believed. Finding the right place for this paranormal crusade was the real trick, for everyone could claim that a night in their basement would *make a believer out of anyone*, but they could never explain why. Those were easy, but finding the most haunted place, that was proving difficult for Tanner.

He asked around, browsed the internet to see if maybe there was one of those silly thrill-seeker listings for paranormal activities. Only one location stuck out, and the more he saw mention of it, the more it interested him. It wasn't somebody's attic, no tourist trap kind of place, and most importantly it wasn't in the middle of a city. It was some nowhere place, a little area of no interest, and it wasn't part of a cemetery, ex-mental hospital or seemingly anything at all. It was listed as a field somewhere in Kentucky.

Most of all, Tanner found that the responses for this area said *not to go*. There were welcoming places for supernatural sightings and paranormal thrill seekers, and then... there was this place. It was noted by enthusiasts as being unpleasant, dangerous and hard to handle. It was no place for photo opportunities. The stories weren't as glamorous. Tanner liked being dissuaded from visiting, relished the challenge, and, even moreso, the history of the area wasn't some fantastic fairy tale of a mad scientist gone wrong, or a young girl murdered. This historic story seemed different, more real. He read into one of the articles with enthusiasm.

"There were many battles fought in the Civil War, big and small, and many infirmaries and medical tents along the sidelines to help those wounded in battle. The casualties were incredible on both sides and injuries often could not be tended to in time, or as efficiently as they needed to be without the wonders of modern medicine. It was an ugly war, nobody thought twice about a certain medical tent with nearly one hundred percent mortality rate. It was passed off as the cost of war.

Nurses in the medical tents were kept busy tending to their current patients, so it was suspicious that one particular nurse named Mary found time to handle that strain, and also assist in delivering food to the combatant soldiers. The Union was losing soldiers left and right, especially within Kentucky. Soldiers that received grievous wounds were susceptible to a wave of epidemic flu, keeping them bedridden and eventually leading to death. The Union responded by sending more troops and hardened officers, but they also inspected the conditions in which these poor soldiers had died.

Nurse Mary was resourceful, and nobody found out about her misdoings until a year after she had wreaked havoc. There was little link between the mysterious deaths, each having dissimilar symptoms, which eventually was discovered that Mary had used over ninety different types of poison and toxins to produce fatal effects. Something of a genius in her own right, the concoctions she fed to Union soldiers were brutal, eventually fatal, and often had a side effect of incredible torment.

Mary's murder count was unknown, and she met her demise on the battlefields from a stray bullet, but rumors state that she was purportedly dealt with by the Union when suspicions arose. Mary was dead, but her disastrous effect crippled the Union war front."

Tanner researched the story further, for validity. Though there were rarely names or locations written, the stories about Southern sympathizers sabotaging the Union armies were strong, and a few had taken place in Kentucky like the story of Mary had claimed. Particular instances seemed to match up. This story had a very good chance of being real.

Now the hard part was finding a way into that field for a night.

The more Tanner looked, the more mysterious this place became. Either people had given up looking for it, or it was truly for the hardcore and nobody else bothered. There was an approximate location outside of a town a mere four hours away from where Tanner currently lived and he considered this a reasonable travel time for such a trip, especially when fueled by worldly spite. For the first time in his practical life, Tanner was going to have an adventure.

The weekend had come and he packed supplies into his car with directions to a motel nearby, wisely assuming that the townsfolk would not easily give up the whereabouts of their haunted treasure, and he would need to stay a while. When he arrived to the motel he found it pleasantly empty and wanting of his patronage. He headed to the front desk, where a bored but cheerful woman with a golden name tag that said "Gloria" was waiting for sparse arrivals.

"What brings you to our town?" she asked with a curious smile.

Tanner decided to try his luck, "To be honest, this is something you could help me with. I've heard a story about a haunted place around here."

She froze midway through handing him his key, "Don't know much about that, I'll say."

"Are you sure?" Tanner asked, gently plucking the key from her hand, "I'm certain it was here."

She hesitated, her motherly country face wracked with worry, "Don't go there. Someone will tell you where it is, but it's not safe."

Gloria shook her head and seemed torn, but didn't say anything else. He decided not to press it, but nodded to her politely, unloaded his few possessions into his room and went outside to find the nearest restaurant for an early dinner.

The town itself was small enough that everything was on the same street, but also big enough that there was a Wal-Mart somewhere down the lane, there was more than one bank, and the diner was a diner because it wanted to be and not because it was the only restaurant in town. Tanner was not a seasoned traveler, but he bet that the diner would house some of the town's local flavor and upon entering, he was correct. Apparently this was also the best place to get meatloaf because every patron seemed to have a plate, and the tables in the mustard-colored room were more full than empty.

"Sit anywhere, hun," was his greeting as he entered, and your most typical diner waitress hustled up to say her hellos, curly burgundy-dyed hair tucked out of her face, and a body that had sampled many of the diner pies. "You're a visitor here, I think? Welcome, I'm Janet. I suggest the meatloaf."

"I noticed," Tanner gestured to the room, "and therefore I will also have the meatloaf. Must be quite special,"

"It's good," she said, not bothering to scribble an order on the pad, "and it's one of the only things Francisco can cook. I'd avoid the eggs Benedict tonight, for one thing."

"Duly noted in case I am dissatisfied with my meatloaf."

Janet smiled at him, aware of his patronizing tone. "Anything to drink?"

"Milk, I'll take a milk," Tanner said, "And also a little gossip, if you're serving that."

Her blue-lidded eyes swept the restaurant conspiratorially, "Look at the size of this town. Gossip's at the top of the menu."

"I was told there was a place," Tanner said, leaning closer to play up the excitement, "a really spooky place around here. You know, haunted."

"You looked like the type," Janet shrugged, eyes unabashedly catching on his thick rimmed glasses and corduroy jacket. "I dunno how much I can tell you."

"It's *that* secret, huh?"

"Let me put in your dinner order." She walked away in strained high heels.

The diner was full of bustle and gravy, quiet conversations of country folk all becoming one big level of noise that seemed just right. Tanner smiled and flipped open his iPad, diddling in a few games and checking the weather for the next few days. Clear. Mild. Uninteresting. The forecast seemed to sniff its displeasure at being used in Kentucky.

"Here's your meatloaf," Janet said, expertly placing the plate on the table, and inexpertly placing the milk between him and the last level of Angry Birds. "Extra veggies 'cause you're scrawny. I got a little of our 'daily special' for you, if you wanna hear it."

"I do."

"The fellow you're after is in that booth in the corner. Name's Jackson, he's a farmer. Don't suggest talking to him right now, as he's just sat down, but someone was gonna tell you anyway. Don't anger him. Just be polite. I added the special onto your tab." Janet placed his bill on the table and sure enough, an extra five dollar charge was on it. "It's customary." And she walked off.

Tanner was amused. The meatloaf was good, for what it was, and he happily paid his bill plus tip before he strode over to the corner booth. "Mr. Jackson?"

Jackson was presumably the man in torn overalls, and he was seated with another fellow, a burlier sort with his badge showing. The officer didn't look like the sort of guy that does active patrol, and he looked up at Tanner and sighed.

Jackson didn't sigh, but the look in his eyes said he wanted to. "Ain't nobody call me Mister that knows me."

"I don't know you, Mister Jackson, not yet," Tanner admitted, "But I also won't waste your time. I heard there was a haunted house around here, and that you might be able to tell me where it is."

Jackson did sigh this time, and his dinner mate said "Don't you let him."

"Why would I bother stoppin' him?" the farmer said.

"It ain't safe. You know that."

Tanner may as well have not been there at all, as the conversation had stopped including him.

Jackson shrugged, "He don't look like one of them loonies."

"That don't stop it being unsafe," the officer said gruffly.

"If I don't tell him, he'll find out and make a mess of it anyway."

"That isn't true," Tanner interjected, "I'm not here to make a mess of anything, or trespass. I'm just here to prove a point. I'd like to spend a night in this so-called haunted house and see for myself."

"We has a skeptic," the burly officer continued to address Jackson exclusively.

Jackson turned to Tanner, "Look, you wanna sleep in a barn, that's your problem but there's all manner of problems in there. Like some recluse spiders, and rottin' wood. It just ain't safe to be inside, might stab your toe on a nail and hurt yourself. I can't be responsible fer that."

"What if I signed a waiver," Tanner pressed, "put it down in writing that any risk I take is my own, that you are not liable for anything that happens to me on your property? We could do something like that."

'With legal counsel," Jackson said with a frown.

"Don't let him do it," said Officer Asshole.

"Legal ain't cheap," Jackson glowered.

"I'll pay for it," Tanner said, "And I'll pay you for the trouble of your time. Including now. Is there a practicing lawyer in town?"

"We could get it cleared with the sheriff," Jackson said, looking across the table.

"You could also get straight to Hell," replied Sergeant Jerkface.

"Barney, this is gonna happen anyhow."

"You can *still* go straight to Hell."

"Barney, I'mma let him."

The policeman crossed his arms, "Then you better ask some other sheriff to give his blessin' on it."

Jackson the farmer threw his hands up, "You're a damn fool sometime. If anythin' happens this means we're all safe and *un-liable*. That's fine by me. As a man of the law-"

"Shut it," the officer said, quelling Jackson with a glance, "I'll sign your damn legal paper but I will also make your wife bake me a pie every week for a damn year for getting' me wrapped up in all this. And I mean it about them pies."

Jackson didn't respond, just looked back up to Tanner, "Come by the police station in the mornin'. Nah, two. Come by then." Then he waved his hand dismissively and centered his attentions on Officer "Safety First" Barney.

Tanner was close, and that felt good. He went cruised along the street in the balmy evening, poked his head into a local library to purchase a cheap, worn copy of *Catcher in the Rye*, and went back to the motel with a smile on his face. He settled into a too-hard bed with bleached-tight sheets, and read a few chapters of the book before resting early. He didn't know what he was getting into, but flesh-eating venomous spiders were probably the worst of it.

In the mornin', he made a few quick stops for provisions, and walked into Farmer Jackson outside the police station. If the man wasn't smoking a pipe, then he had the attitude of one who did, so much so that Tanner imagined him doing it as they talked.

"Had a little discussion of rent, as I see it." Farmer Jackson looked past him into the street. "You'd be lookin' at a night, ya said, so I think compensation could be around the three hundred mark. Just to make it clear, you're technically rentin' my equipment, bein' as it's a barn, so we'll have another thing fer ya to sign. With cash if you ain't mindin'. We like cash here."

"I have more than enough on me currently to handle it.

"Good." He stopped. "You sleepin' through the night?"

"I have little intention of it, actually."

"You'll sleep. Just... I hesitate to tell ya to pick up a cot, but..."

"I think a cot will do nicely."

"Might wanna be off the floor. Yer call. Hardware store's to the left a ways. Pick up a few 'lectric lanterns if stayin' awake's whatcha want. Gets dark in there. You afraid of bats? Well you ain't afraid of anythin' you said. There's bats. Nothin' you can do about 'em, just deal with the flappin'." Jackson shrugged once more, "Might get a little cold. Get a jacket over that sorry excuse for a flannel shirt. Might get a hat as well. You know the rest."

"I'll do all those things," Tanner nodded at him, "Lanterns, cot, jacket, hat."

Jackson snuffled an agreement then pointed him to the store. A quick trudge down the street and a hefty purchase later, Tanner's arms were laden as he met back up with Jackson, sitting on a bench, appearing simultaneously pensive and casual.

"Let's get ya signed up," was all he said as he entered the police building one more time.

They were waved into a glass office, which held Officer Barney's bulk and signature scowl.

"Good afternoon," Tanner said, carefully placing a supermarket bakery pie on the desk. "It's likely not as good as Mrs. Jackson's pies, but I wanted to make sure you receive payment early."

Barney grunted, looking sour, even moreso with the apparent good will of some punk kid.

"We've been discussing the legal issues," Jackson said, looking tired. "We have a draft written, it ain't a perty thing but it'll do for what we want. Take a look."

Barney leaned backwards at a backbreaking angle to snatch a warm paper out of the printer, sliding it across the desk towards Tanner, his eyes trying to avoid and finally resting on the pie.

"What kind is it."

"Pecan."

"Hmph."

Tanner read over the list, which seemed thorough, but inexpertly written. Included were things like mental distress, all injury including but not limited to environmental, natural, spider bites, wood, and self-inflicted ailments, loss of consciousness, asthma attacks, any pre-existing conditions that flare up, and the list went on. He looked it over, unfazed, and heard Jackson add, "What about that other fella. The Smith kid."

The sheriff plunked away at the keyboard for a moment and a new sheet was printed out, updated to include "amnesia."

"Could shorten some stuff," Barney grumbled, "categorize. It'll take a bit longer."

"I ain't picky," Jackson said, taking another look at the document, "this'll cover me?"

"Ayup."

"You ready, kid?"

The contract was passed along the desk by a stony-faced sheriff, and Jackson watched soberly as Tanner scribbled his name, no sounds but the scratching of a pen and rustle of papers. The second page, a rental agreement, was placed in front of him, and a stack of twenty dollar bills appeared on the desk. A nod passed between the silent group. Slowly Jackson rose from his seat, joints creaking audibly, and Tanner followed obediently, hoping he could appease the man further.

The air outside was crisp. Evening was approaching early. "Suppose you'll wanna see it tonight," the reluctant farmer said, protectively clutching the billfold in his pocket.

"I would," Tanner replied, "Shall I collect my things and follow your car?"

Jackson sniffled and avoided eye contact. "...Ayup."

The weathered barn was visible from whatever main road they had come in on, but at first glance, it looked no different than any other barn in a rural town. As they pulled to the side of the road, Tanner noticed uncharacteristically aggressive fencing surrounding the land from the street, suggesting value within. The farmer unlocked a great gate, and their cars plunged along an overgrown path leading to the lone structure of the field.

They parked the cars some distance away.

"I'll leave the gate unlocked for ya. Just in case yer hankerin' to leave, no g'bye necessary."

They stepped through the thigh-high grass to inspect the barn, the sagging doors perpetually open and dug into the ground. It looked plain and lonely in the fading light, with no interesting features except for the parts that had fallen into disrepair. The structure wasn't quite on its last legs, but it surely could no longer serve as a barn.

Jackson was muttering off bits of advice as they came to him, "Might be some wildlife about. I don't just mean rabbits or the like. Stay away from fungus. Don't try and tame any snakes or what have you. Just be safe. Got yer lights? Think you should be set. I'll check up on you come mornin' time. Not too early."

"Thank you for your help."

Jackson grunted a noncommittal reply and started towards the door. "Good luck." Then sighed, "You damn fool."

The barn was old, and smelled of rotting wood. The most imminent danger appeared to be in the whole place caving in on Tanner in the night, though it would take quite the gust to propel the structure into motion. The grass on the ground was far shorter than the field outside, but enough to tickle his ankles as it crept under his pants, and threatened to overtake the edges of the cot Tanner had erected. He placed electric lanterns around the empty stalls and walls, staying mostly close to him for the greatest area of light, a few nestled in the grass, projecting leafy shapes to the walls and ceiling. All in all, it wasn't so bad, a dirty little rundown shack where he would spend his night. Makes for an interesting story whether anything happens at all. He felt refreshed by a childlike sense of adventure, where he would sleep in strange places just to do it. Twilight was creeping in and Tanner decided against music, in case he missed some unearthly moans or rattling chains or whatever people classified as terrifying.

Tanner read in the lamplight, his attention sustained by the Catcher in the Rye as he waited for anything interesting to happen. Anything at all. After a few hours, he sipped an energy drink daintily as the chill crept in from the edges of the barn. His jacket was warm and unfashionable. He had bought a blanket but it wasn't as useful as it claimed to be in the bag. He sipped, and read, and vaguely enjoyed the solace of the night around him.

Tanner awoke with a start.

What?

He didn't even remember falling asleep, or even having the temptation to do so. How ridiculous. The energy drink was still clutched in his hand, not a drop had been spilled. Perhaps he hadn't been out longer than a moment, and the drowsing had made him spasm as he drifted off... but really, he didn't feel tired at all. He pulled out his phone, attempting to browse Twitter over an archaic satellite internet connection, then pulled out his tablet to see if that connection had better luck. It was ten o'clock and the only danger he felt was the imminent fear of dying from boredom. His eyes moved to looking around the empty, lamp-lit barn some more. Really, it wasn't so bad.

He jerked again.

This time he immediately looked at his phone, which showed eleven. Maybe he was sleepier than he thought. It had been a rather grueling day with all the small town diplomacy to maneuver. Another energy drink could be in order, he thought, since he'd like to last most of the night without sleeping, but... he could concede to a nap in the future if his body insisted. Tanner fiddled with his iPad again, but the screen was black. Perhaps it was just asleep like he had been, but no amount of rousing would make it turn back on. Of all the days for the thing to malfunction, it had to pick the night he was reliant on entertainment. That also meant, due to the lack of power outlets in a field, that he shouldn't be overusing his phone either....

Tanner sighed, idly thumbing the pages of the book in his hands. He should have brought a second clock. People never wear watches anymore, but now would have been a great opportunity. He took a few pieces of beef jerky from his pack and sat back in his chair to finish his book, only the last quarter of it to go. It was a rather quick book, Tanner remembered too late, but he also wouldn't be tearing through it so fast if his electronics worked.

A wind blew through the barn, soft, but making a slow whistling.

The canvas of the tent flapped in the breeze, rippling above him in the dying light, such sterile white that he could nearly see through it when the sun shone at angles. It smelled rank of death and something wrong that was worse. Not like that sanitary tang of sickness on the breeze, this smelled like lost hope and infection. He shivered in the cold that may not have been at all environmental, and heard the moans, the loud gasps of pain of the others around him that his eyes were too glassy to see. He saw the moving shapes, some twitching, some pitching back and forth beneath restraints for an invisible torture they were undergoing. The noise, the

utter endless yells of agony; where one stopped, another pitch started up
like a symphony.

The noise in his throat died as he awoke, and realized he was the one yelling. He was startled, he admitted to himself, but that gave way to puzzlement and eventually he rolled his eyes. Just a bad dream. I'm just getting the best of myself, he thought. He was not good at imagination and this would be a silly time to begin. He adjusted in his seat, and decided to take a piss break just for a little walk. The barn doors were uncomfortably nearby so he opted to pee in a far corner of the vast building, relieved again by the male's ability to make bodily functions so convenient. What a silly night for dreaming, Tanner thought, and inwardly blamed the caffeine drinks for getting his mind too wound up. He cranked up his lawn chair to an uncomfortably upright position and once again opened his book to read. The clock on his phone read twelve-thirty. He must have drifted for a while.

There was pain. It was slow and warm like the heat of a fever, then cold and sharp for only a second. It slowed to an ache, spreading everywhere in Tanner's body, and he became aware of his breathing being slow, exhausted, wheezing. He rolled to his side on his rigid cot, shivering away the pain to lock eyes with his nearest bedmate. He was two feet from Tanner, hanging skeletally off the edge of his bunk, staring. The face was drained of blood and most else, pupils so tiny they hardly existed, mouth agape and purplish, the only splash of color about him. His hair was mostly gone, wispy and white from what must have been extended strain, and he lay dead with a blank, long face of abandonment and suffering. He had lost all semblance of humanity but the empty look of shock. Mesmerized in death.

Two larger men came from the corner of Tanner's eye and got a grip on the body, sharing the burden, the frame bending easily between them, and as the head lolled back face skyward, it began to laugh, a high pitched maniacal cackle that affected no other part of the body but the mouth, and the bloodless eyes bugged with the strain of it. The two men kept walking out of the tent. The skeletal figure croaked its death cry all the way.

How did he get on the cot? Tanner sat straight up, body covered haphazardly by a sleeping bag. He had been sitting in that chair. He was awake. He was reading. Then he was in the cot, lying. Maybe he had been overcome by sleep, so that he just couldn't recall getting ready for bed. But surely he could have crawled inside the bag instead of placing it on top of him. The caffeine was making him jittery and feel a bit ill, he wondered if this trip was good for him. Maybe he was catching a cold, visiting new places can wreak havoc on your immune system. It was chilly and a breeze had picked up, he put his hat on a little tighter and considered settling onto the cot, giving up on staying awake when his body was rebelling so fervently. At least in his sleep, the night would pass faster. He took off his shoes and crawled into the sleeping bag, clothed.

Some cots were higher than the rest. It gave a good view of what was going on close by, from his space nearer to the floor. Tanner stared down past his feet, eyes watering with a resurgence of the sharp, biting pain that seemed to be all over. Through his welled up vision, he saw the cot closest to him.

The nurses were out of restraints, and this man's fingernails bit into his scalp to rip fine shreds down through his forehead, clumps of hair hanging limp from strings of skin. This changed nothing. He continued to scream, his eyes rolled back into his head, fingers reconnecting to descend down his face, catching on his eyelids and tearing away a flap, oblivious to the damage. The screams were muffled, resigned moans that seemed to change pitch according to misery more than pain.

A white skirt and legs interrupted Tanner's view, charging towards his own bunk. She was larger than he thought she would be, and appeared to be in her thirties. Her face was bulb-nosed and bulgy, expressing a hardness that must come standard with working in this environment. Her hand pressed into Tanner's stomach, easing him into a flatter position as she yanked to tighten a tourniquet he had not noticed on his leg. He could not feel his leg at all. There appeared to be nothing wrong with it at a glance, but Mary unsheathed a vicious looking syringe. "Medicine," she said, and with a dull look, she inserted it professionally into his leg, which he could not feel. She pulled out and brandished the syringe for a moment, her only truly human movement, and gave the slightest hint of a lopsided smile. Then the pain hit again, stronger and colder than before. He screamed and he saw her pat him on the leg he couldn't feel. "It'll get better."

His leg was tangled tight at an odd angle, combination of pants and sleeping bag creating a restriction which he thrashed against, and it took a few panicked minutes to undo. He flopped himself onto the barn floor and into the sparse, bristly grass, his body weight making his numb leg crumple. Ridiculous idea, he thought as he sat himself at the edge of his cot, ridiculous dreams, ridiculous thoughts. All of it was just.... but he never finished that thought. Tanner shuddered away his visions and decided that sleep was not a good idea. Clearly he was getting sick, or something was bothering him.

The reception on his cell phone was blinking in and out, not even enough to send a warm text message to his girlfriend or a few of the boys, and the clock read a little past four. The night was nearly over so at least he'd be spared many more nightmares due to his own idiocy. Tanner wondered if leaving now wasn't a good idea, but the path to the car was dark and his stuff would be hard to gather in the depth of the barn. He tried his iPad one more time, tapping on the screen and trying some fidgeting to get his mind off things. The *Catcher in the Rye* was missing, probably lost in some nearby clump of grass. Yes, it was all good for a story, getting pneumonia and having fever dreams in a barn in the Kentucky countryside. He sneered at his reflection, pale and sickly on the glossy black surface of his tablet.

The metallic stench was awful and he didn't see why nobody went to stop it. The man was straining at his joints, bending his body out of shape in ways that suggested dislocation, his eyes mad and red like a rabid dog. Tanner watched him.

The arm was wet with blood but not enough to disguise the tuberous loose ends of veins, the whiteness of ligaments stretched tight, strings of fresh flesh torn by teeth anatomically ill-made for such use. The man dug his face in and gnawed, until the space between his the radius and ulna bones was visible, and bits of meat fell to the floor with a wet slap. He bit down on his own bones and cried, closed his eyes and Tanner realized how much more human he looked, restrained and helpless against the pain, even to end it. Tanner's own pain was worsening, until he couldn't keep his eyes open, especially as he saw a white skirt stretched over wide hips, clearing a path to approach his cot.

He was on his knees. Somewhere. In a stall perhaps. Where was his jacket? His sleeve was torn off. There was blood. There was more blood than he had thought for anything. Drops of it splashed at his jeans, his left forearm scraped deep, the wound oozing and lined with spindly splinters of wood, shucked off the jagged hunk of wood held in Tanner's right hand.

There was blood. So much.

His throat was sore and his head felt feverish. He stood to move but his leg was still numb, inexplicably. He pitched forward and found enough energy and coordination to walk, leaving as quickly as he could, dropping the bloodied scrap of wood at his feet as he left everything, nothing mattered but his keys and the car.

Tumbling, hobbling into the morning dew, the first vestiges of light in the sky creating a grey-blue aura all around him, Tanner reached his vehicle and started up, pressing the pedals with his left foot and pushing the gate open with the bumper of his car, driving up the road until he could see the motel. His back pocket held his wallet. His keys were in the ignition. His phone, sputtering with lack of battery life, was in his pocket. Everything else was replaceable.

He drove past the motel, and kept on down the highway which he hoped is where he came from. Maybe he'd stop to rest. Maybe there'd be a bottle of cheap whiskey waiting for him, or some cough medicine.

Whatever happened, he wanted to be far away.

IX.

So many people asked why Mr. Anderson didn't retire, but they knew the answer was that he was too good to leave. Some teachers, no matter where they are, remain exceptional and change lives forever. Mr. Anderson was one of those people. He made students learn English, whether they wanted to or not, and succeeded in making them enthusiastic about going to class. His curriculum was solid and his teaching style was force-feeding medicine during a comedy show. He was sharp in his age, and didn't look to be as old as he must have been. Anderson stood tall in body and mind, his praise was genuine and supportive, but he also was a sort of high school celebrity. He owned his classroom like a city-state and when you spoke, you knew you were in the presence of a great man, a clever man, someone who was respected and left well alone. It was like he spoke in fluent MLA format. He existed to teach this job, this class, at this school.

Every year the educational board enticed him with a new retirement package, but nobody knew why they tried. The school itself would be worse without him. The students would be robbed of an experience, and deprived of begrudging knowledge of correct apostrophe usage. They liked his style, they didn't always get his humor and, a lot of the time, they just went about their business. Yet, certain students really took to him, when he would say such off-kilter statements as, "Have a good weekend, don't molest small animals."

Maybe nobody cared. Daisy cared. She laughed and wrote what he said down on her notebook, got to class early to hang out sometimes, genuinely thinking she had a lot to learn from this man who was one of the most notable people at the school. She sat rapt as he played part of the *War of the Worlds* radio play, and was the first to return her permission slip to see *The Crucible* at a local theatre. He would sometimes get waylaid in his lectures about literature and the times, his mellifluous voice describing the impact of a book, the culture behind a generation or even sometimes just thoughts. He never analyzed a story singularly, he would paint the backdrop of its creation and the impact it had at the time, giving the full picture to his students so they could envision it for themselves and see why it changed the world. It didn't always work... high school is high school. Then there were a few kids like Daisy who wanted to come back and listen all over again.

It was easy to be star struck, in Daisy's case. She was an intelligent girl, not just in terms of book smarts and dedication but a cleverness that made school easy and subsequently boring. She wanted to learn more than what was offered in books, and when working on projects or writing a sonnet in Mr. Anderson's class, she found she was exercising that part of education she was lacking. There was a fullness to his teaching. Not just memorization, but understanding. Plus he would sometimes put on Miles Davis albums quietly while grading tests and, to her, that felt right. Something was right. Lutes and harpsichords during Shakespeare, Jazz during *The Great Gatsby*; learning could be environmental, and a lot more than just words.

She was a pretty good writer, though it wasn't her passion: she wanted to be a singer. Writing was a part of that, but she valued choir more than English, and so compliments fell on deaf ears. Mr. Anderson had often pulled her aside for words of encouragement, trying to guide this young soul in a direction where it would be remarkable.

It would only be a few months until she graduated and danced off into the real world beyond, with promises of distant colleges and fair scholarships that might challenge her more than a tiny school in a boring place like this. She began to take her friendship with Mr. Anderson more seriously, and really value what was being given to her every time she stepped into that special classroom.

His lectures meant more. In a class of seventeen- and eighteen-year-olds, he was the only person she wanted to know more about. It was all the little things he said that caught her off guard, the bits of genius nobody appreciated. As he debated with an angry mob of teenagers about what constituted a real rhyme, Mr. Anderson would reply, "Close only counts in horseshoes, hand grenades, atomic warfare *and love.*"

It was just the way he said it. He was a powerful person.

And he was teaching high school English class.

"Finals are coming up, with the speed of a freight train, from your blind side," he said as he passed out study guides down the rows of desks. "Yes, summer is getting closer but there's that one last pain in the ass, and you probably need to get an 'A' on it. I'll have a study session this Thursday after school, a big one lasting as long as we need it to. I'm even bringing coffee. It's not good coffee though, so I have some flavored creamer to take the edge off. We'll sit down like skittish rodents and learn about literature."

Daisy was mentally clearing her Thursday already.

It was a big crowd for the after-school kids took up almost the whole classroom with a last ditch effort to make sure they passed, or at least answered a question or two correctly. They were mostly poindexters who had nothing to fear, and a few panicked sorts whose enthusiasm quickly deteriorated, and by five half of the group was gone. The other half were doing loud pop quizzes, sipping coffee and feeling like adults. Daisy called out a few answers here and there and refilled her tea, hoping to be the last one there. By seven, the students were leaving and she made the excuse that her mom would only be available after eight. Mr. Anderson paid her no mind until the room was empty.

"Oh, the entertainment's all gone," he said wryly, noticing her, "the study session isn't graded on attendance, you can leave whenever you like."

"No, I just," Daisy stumbled over her words a little, "I don't get picked up until a little later. You don't mind me trespassing here for a bit?"

He nodded, "*Mi casa es su casa.* I'd be here anyway. The wife's on a business trip so I am not being badgered to come home before midnight."

"...You wouldn't stay that late would you?"

"The acoustics in this room are much better than my living room," he said, taking a seat at his tall desk and flipping through a stack of papers, "Sometimes I put on some Dave Brubeck and enjoy the evening. That's what the armchair is for." He held a paper up to his appraising eye, "And reading terrible essays."

"Why don't you put on some music now?" Daisy suggested, "I don't mean to be a bother."

"I suppose you could do it for me. Go switch on the radio there. Whatever CD is in the top should suffice. I'm not feeling picky unless you are."

Delicate horn melodies met her ears. "What is this?"

Mr. Anderson paused momentarily, tilting his head to the ceiling, "Ah, the harmonious tones of Lester Young. Listen and be amazed." He looked back at his stack of papers and frowned, "Anything you need help with while you're here?"

"I was going to ask the same thing."

He smirked, "Much as I trust your ability, I don't consider it wise to have you grading the papers of your brethren, when the answers are so subjective. Oftentimes I am tempted to cover the answers with angry frowny faces over and over until I feel better, or they learn of my displeasure."

Daisy looked stricken, "Is it really so bad?"

"Not at all," he said, looking at her over his glasses, "But I shouldn't be seeing the word 'bro' in any response relating to iambic pentameter."

"That's well deserving of a frowny face."

"I think..." he paused, "I need a break. So talk to me. Finals are approaching, what is in store for the talented Miss Daisy?"

She smiled and took her time to think. It had been keeping her up at night, a whole future she didn't know yet. "I don't know what just yet. There's a few colleges I've been accepted to, out of state. I'm really looking forward to it. I even was accepted to one because of the essay you helped me with."

"Is that so? Well you deserve it. And not just because I helped."

"No I wouldn't have made it so well if not for your input," she rushed, and clasped her hands together in her lap, "I'm a little afraid now because school is such a safe place and when I have questions... I won't know where to go."

"That's the thing about teachers," Mr. Anderson said, resting his pencil on his chin, "we always want to help, and teach. So if you ever need a helping hand, you know where to find us. Plus college will be full of helpful old sods like myself who will trip over themselves to help you become a greater writer."

"You're not tripping over yourself, that's my job. I'm the teenager."

"You'd be surprised. We see talent and we can't help but fawn. It's as though we teach school year in and year out just to see the two or three students who are bound to be something in the future. Definitely the most inspiring part of being up there."

Daisy looked at this older, greying man who had spent so much time in an overly-decorated classroom, "Why did you get started teaching?"

"Because I was good at it."

"Is that *why* you teach?"

Mr. Anderson looked at the ceiling for a moment, "I teach for many reasons, and I think it's a civic sense of duty as much as anything. I don't want to put frownies on the paper. I want to see that troubled kid get A's and surprise himself. Maybe surprise me too. It's happened. There's a challenge to imparting knowledge onto a reluctant audience."

"You do really well at it. I know people are learning even if they don't want to. I think you're the best teacher here."

"Well I'm very flattered to hear that, because students like yourself make teaching a lot more satisfying," he said. "I've said it before but I think you have a great future ahead of you. I can't wait to see how that plays out."

Daisy flushed, the warmth of her face matched by the warmth in her chest, "It'll be a lot of luck. Maybe I'll be a songwriter."

"They bring in the money! I don't want to blame you for the catchy lyrics behind a pop star's hit though," he looked down at her over the black rims of his glasses again.

"I'll try to be as surreptitious as possible."

"You used a vocabulary word."

"I like it."

"Me too."

Silence fell between them and Daisy looked at him from her station, a student-sized desk looking up at the behemoth podium where he did his work. It was being in the shadow of a benevolent mountain.

"You didn't... really answer... why you started teaching," she pried.

"It's a long and old story, and a boring one just like me."

"You're not boring," she said, "please tell it!"

He shrugged, "Well, I liked reading, I liked understanding the impact of the reading, and eventually I became good at showing that to others."

"That wasn't very long. Where did you grow up?"

"In a lot of places, seeing a lot of things. Books were one of the only constants, and I regard them as friends even now. Then I share these friends."

"You went to school a lot, I guess?" She wondered what that was like. In her head, college was a grand place with tall cathedral buildings and ties. She thought about Mr. Anderson as a student himself, and how different that would be. She imagined darker hair, a youthful face... her mind wandered.

"I have been to so many universities, I can hardly tell them apart," Mr. Anderson answered, "I learned valuable lessons about how to teach and how not to. If I can remember by now... and I think that's what really got me started teaching. Plus I had more than enough paperwork to tell me I was qualified, and the school district agreed."

Now she imagined him as a young teacher, "Have you taught anywhere else?"

"Just here, just in this classroom. If I'm lucky, I'll stay here a lot longer." His fingers drummed along with the rhythm of the jazz around them, and he hummed a bit of the melody. Daisy thought, maybe he doesn't want to talk about it... but she couldn't see any reason why that would be. So she kept asking.

"What else did you do before?"

Mr. Anderson counted them off on his fingers, "Some journalism, as all writers and critics do. Worked in a few bookshops, libraries and publishing companies, like all the bibliophiles. An ice cream stand in the fifties."

She laughed, "Why the ice cream stand?"

"I got to look at pretty ladies on the boardwalk. It was a good summer gig," he said with a smile.

Daisy looked at the whiteboard, full of vocabulary words and crossed-out examples, "I've never even had a job before. I want one, they seem… adult."

"They seem *adult*?"

"They do!" she perked up, "like, a token of independence, a paycheck, first step of freedom! It's so exciting, the next step in life."

Mr. Anderson looked at her, "I guess it's been so long since I've considered it that way, I've forgotten. Thank you for that refreshing viewpoint."

"You keep in touch with so many current things, how do you do it?"

"I think I stay tapped into the youth just by being around them so much. Osmosis of Not Lameness. I'm not personally cool by any means."

Daisy shook her head, "You don't need to be cool. You're amazing."

He laughed, "Well that, I mean, thank you. For an old guy that's a pretty nice compliment. Let's hope you stay cool enough for the both of us."

"Oh, I'm not cool either. I wouldn't be at school at night if I was. I think."

It sounded ruder than she meant, and she started to try to amend her statement when he stopped her with a wave of his hand, "Smart people aren't usually cool until later, don't worry. Someday you'll be a successful twenty-something and everyone will regret they called you a nerd once. Even if they didn't. Do you get called that?"

"No. They don't pay attention at all."

"They'll regret that too."

Daisy bit her lip, clasping her hands under the desk again. Those little thoughts kept crawling around in her mind. "I just… don't know if I'm going to be successful outside my safety net. And you keep telling me how great I am, but I feel like I'm twelve."

He rested his chin on his hand to look at her, "Keep that feeling. When you're twenty-five you'll feel like you're eighteen. It's good to keep a youthful perspective."

"But I want help."

"You'll always have it if you ask, you know."

"From you?"

Mr. Anderson looked at her seriously from the heights of importance, "I will do my best."

"You'll forget."

"I rarely forget."

And she got that flushed feeling again, her words betrayed her. "I don't know what I'd do without you."

Mr. Anderson shook his head, "It's just the next big step, it's normal to feel that way. I have coached many a high school senior into their new lives in college."

"College seems stupid somehow," she said, her frustration rising as she stared at her desk, "It's like all the classes out there won't make me worthy of being anything but a student to you, when I just want to be a friend."

He was solemn. "You don't have to earn friendship with a degree."

The words poured out like inner poison, "But I'm years behind, and *stupid*, and you have all this life that you talk about and I can't think of *what* I could offer anything in return. Potential just isn't enough. I don't feel like I'll be enough to be considered an equal and that's intimidating and angering because more than anything, I want to impress you as much as you have impressed me. I want to be important to you. Because I'll always remember your classes and the impact you had on all of us."

He let her speak, then soberly stood up to take the seat behind her. She twisted in her chair, and Daisy saw the wrinkles of his aged face a bit more clearly with only a few feet of desk and soulful jazz between them. He looked away across the room for a moment, seeming to gather his thoughts. She was breathless.

"Eventually you might learn this, but now is as good a time as any," he said, his dark brown eyes finding hers, "I can't just attribute your blowup to nerves, but I can assure you, you are important to me, and I do want to see a young person do well. I think, from a certain position, that I can keep assisting in your work if you need it, supporting if you want it, and cheering from the sidelines even when you move on without me. I'll keep an eye out, for as long as I'm around. That... will be a long time."

"Long enough?" she asked reflexively, "My grandparents are already harping on me to have children before they're gone. It's just so much pressure on a timetable that isn't mine."

"....First, apt as it may be, direct comparison to your grandparents is a little bit rude." He chuckled as she blushed, "An old guy doesn't like being reminded of his age. I forget how much time passes while my nose is in textbooks all day. Answer is, a lot. Now, all I can say about other people's schedules is... they're not important. Take all the time you want, to be whomever you want. If it's anything I can attest to, I will be there when you crystallize in life, even if neither of us know how, yet. No matter how long it takes you."

Daisy felt serious, overwhelmed and touched. Her head was a mess, and she opened her mouth to sort it out but had nothing to say yet. "What if it takes fifty years."

"What of it?"

"You're not my age."

"I could be."

She scowled, suddenly apprehensive, "Are you talking about reincarnating?"

"I'm talking about something very special and very secret."

"Is it religion?"

"Of course not," and his scowl matched hers, "You know how I deal with those kooks."

Daisy smirked, "You introduce them to your holy Campbell's soup can."

"I pray to it every night. Keeps me healthy."

"But I don't understand."

"None understand the ways of the Campbell's soup can."

"I meant..."

"I know."

Mr. Anderson took off his black-rimmed glasses, the same style as the hip kids wore. In her eyes, he wore them better. His voice sounded quieter now, weighted.

"I have ways of staying around, that I don't know if anyone else has. Someone must. Maybe they're off teaching history to teenagers on a mountain somewhere. Just as boring of a life as I lead. But maybe that's why we're around, to help others.

He leaned forward, and they were only a foot apart, "I'm not proclaiming I have the wisdom of the ages, but if it's one thing I can boast, it's a longevity you can't get with another mentor. It may run out any day, any minute or hour, because I don't know what it is better than anyone else does. I just *know* that I'll see you at your first book signing, or broadway play, or anything you choose if you find your way to it."

She watched as his eyes fell to the desk, and he leaned back. "I've lived a few lives by now, and I'm not lying about that. Is it any wonder why I made you all read *The Once And Future King*? Merlyn said it better than I could, and I've had a few lifetimes to make it sound prettier. T.H. White beat me to the punch. I'm no magician, but I've finally found what I think I was meant to work on in the world. It only took me three tries."

Daisy was stark still, trying to understand what he was saying. "You... come back?"

"Somehow, I never leave."

"You're screwing with me. Just 'cause I'm a kid."

"I wouldn't, I respect you more than that," and the solid gaze was there again, without the impediment of glasses, "I would much rather prove it than talk about it anyway. I'm patient."

The silliness of the thought struck her as she was already saying it. "What if I could go with you?"

"How do you mean." He was serious again, eyebrows closing together.

"If you could... teach me?" Daisy's voice quivered, "If we could continue as long as we needed, together..."

"I couldn't teach it to a dog, I hardly know what does it."

"We can learn," she sputtered, "we can find out-"

"We can't, Daisy, and I wouldn't expect it of you either. You have a life you must live without giving thought to mine. Luckily, I will be able to see you along your journey. I can even attend your wedding someday."

"I don't want a wedding. I want to achieve with you."

His gaze narrowed, "If you're suggesting what I think you-"

"Yes."

And there was quiet. His eyes were steely and hers were eager, enamored with this spirit she saw before her.

"...Daisy, you're just a child."

"I won't always be."

"And I will *always* be a crotchety old man. No matter the new life I lead."

"I like anything that you are."

There was a hint of a sigh, "This is... flattering, truly it is, and I'm not saying that you are not quite the impressive woman-"

"—You just called me a child—"

"—But you still have much to see in the world," he explained, "And this will seem *much* less important to you."

"I don't want it to!"

"To be clear, you don't know what you want."

It was frigid and it hit her like ice. Her thoughts were all rushed and unclear, and a person she respected and... even loved, had sent her spinning.

"Daisy, you have a whole life ahead of you. For now, just the one." Mr. Anderson was pleading, which made him seem tired, "Don't waste it chasing old men who are too prudish to accept the incredible gift of your affection. It's late, and there's little more to say than that."

He stood up and she stood with him, slight next to his large frame, looking young and spooked. Daisy gathered her things, quiet in her shame, listening to the stereo go mute. Watching as the classroom door was shut and locked. They walked outside into the darkness of the evening, bound by tension, and a few short steps to the parking lot where a welcoming pair of tail lights were waiting.

"Daisy, focus on what you have right now, and I'll see you at the finish line."

Mr. Anderson nodded, put on a handsome old style fedora that only older men can wear, and began his walk to his car.

"Then what?"

He stopped, "Exactly. Then what?"

In the car, her mother asked her how the study session went. Daisy replied, "I think I'm going to pass," and burst into tears.

X.

$\mathscr{I}rma$

ANYONE WOULD HAVE BEEN JOLTED BY THE CAR ACCIDENT. IRMA heard the screeching brakes and leapt around. It was close enough to fear for herself, close enough to see the headlights sweeping the sidewalk next to her, close enough to see the body stuck beneath that car. Everything went foggy and white. She lost her breath and sat on the pavement in shock. Her account of the accident was recorded to the police, she was given some coffee and cut loose, but she had awful dreams of headlights. In her dreams, she was the one under the car.

A year passed of the same recurring dreams and she fought to convince herself that she could never have been under that car, that it was her fear and regret plaguing her. The girl who died was of similar age and her life ended so quickly, Irma was still shaken by the realization of mortality. She would sometimes get flashes of another life, the life the girl might have had, and dismissed them as being nervous, stupid thoughts. It was just the guilt at not being able to have done more.

Until one day.

Irma was staring into a window of a store, and had been for an hour. Just standing, looking in at a display that caught her. It wasn't that she liked it, or wanted it, but there was a strange familiarity. A few passersby asked her if she needed help with anything. She smiled and shook her head, but her eyes returned, glassy, to the display.

It was too early for Christmas anyway, October was time for Halloween, but that wasn't what glued her to the window. The ornaments twinkled on their window display, tiered platforms of heirloom ornaments showcased through the years and available for purchase once more, because when creativity falters, you just go with what you know. Hallmark had resurrected retired tree ornaments, and with it, resurrected a memory.

It was a stupid, cute, little white mouse sitting in a tart cup. It made no sense. It wasn't even Christmas-y. But she stared for fifty minutes straight, and then she understood why. She had to sit down.

She had it before. It was her favorite.

Her family is Jewish.

But she put it on a tree. And she wouldn't let it be packed away with the rest of the ornaments, so eventually her mother convinced her father to let her keep it out all year long.

Her mother and father were divorced.

She had hung it up on a post in the loft bedroom she had in the fourth grade, which made her like the house a lot better than the other one they had just moved from, on the mountain.

Irma had lived in the city all her life.

Melissa hadn't.

Her whole body felt jittery. Irma stayed there for another hour, then purchased the mouse ornament and went home.

She twiddled the ornament in her fingers, skipping dinner to lie down, trying to jump start the slow process of remembering, and making sense of what she found. After a few hours, she began to cry.

Melissa started waking up from her shock, and her sleep.

Over the next few months, Irma began keeping a diary (like Melissa used to do) documenting all the things she could remember, why she felt them, and what it could mean. She played with the little mouse ornament on her side table before bed, her parents hadn't asked about it, and she hadn't told them or anyone. It was hard to be sure, but she had faith in what she felt, that she had memories from another person. She started doing research and playing little games with herself to coax out new information, even unsuccessfully tried to use an Ouija board. What was her last name? What did she look like? What was this life she left behind?

She had been in high school, but a different one than this, probably a few towns over though she couldn't remember the name, and she had lived all sorts of places besides that, like the mountain

72

she couldn't remember either. She recalled things at times that made no sense, like a certain flavor of Lip Smackers lip balm that gave her a headache, or the name of a pet she had when she was twelve years old. Whiskers. Why? Was any of this relevant? Was she supposed to dig deeper into these flimsy details and extract a life she had?

Irma considered that it could be multiple personality disorder, or some kind of strange spiritual malady, but she didn't dare get help for it because it felt like there was no help to get. She was flustered but not hurt, and she was not two people. She was one, just both. Simultaneously. Her head tried to wrap around it and still couldn't grasp what it was or could have been, nor was there any way to learn more about the life there once was. She sang along with Christmas carols, but everyone did whether they were Jewish or not, and even tried some egg nog. Irma visited her friends with their Christmas trees and watched Rudolph and Frosty the Snowman, but only got small shimmers of memory... a snow globe that sang Silent Night, and the first night in a bed with fresh flannel sheets, the best sleep of her former life.

What did it mean? Among these displaced memories and residual feelings, the holiday passed in a blur of intangible details and Irma went back to her next college semester with a few less classes, and a lot less confidence in how the world worked. At least she had gained better vocabulary in the meantime. It's the little perks of... of what exactly?

The grocery line was slow and Irma was tired that night, getting back from a lab a few towns away. She knew her mom would be home late, so she bought herself a salad and some energy drinks for the next study weekend, collected her receipt and was ready to walk out the door when her eyes reflexively snapped to the checkout lines, hearing something familiar.

"Thank you Mrs. Martin."

That was all. But she revolved on the spot and saw....

...Was that her?

God, she looked like hell.

Her hair was thinner and her wrinkles were deeper, but it had only been a few years. She was clutching two large cans of cat food, a roasted chicken and a far larger bottle of vodka, they were helping her put it into the bag after the last one split up the side. Without thinking about consequences, Irma walked over.

"Hello, Mrs. Martin."

The woman looked up, slightly annoyed, as she grasped her plastic bag, "Hello?"

"Crazy seeing you here! I uh," she struggled to breathe, "I was a good friend of Melissa's."

She used the word 'was.' Melissa had died. Irma had forgotten.

Mrs. Martin, Jan in fact, was in front of her, nodding away. She looked a little sad, but she tried to crack a smile, "It's been a while since we've seen her! Both!"

Irma tried to laugh but it was breathy and horrified, as Melissa recoiled inwardly from a strange joke at her expense. "It has. I'm sorry, you may not recognize me, I'm Irma. I remember you from," she hesitated, "picking Melissa up from soccer practice a few times. I have a mind for faces!"

"Yep." Mrs. Martin was trying to look busy.

"Well, how's everything going? The rest of the family....?" Irma trailed off, not knowing what to ask or say.

"Fine. All fine. George and I split, but that's fine 'cause I found another fella who knows what a real woman is, you know?" Jan let out another bawdy laugh, unbecoming of her, and Irma could smell alcohol on her breath. "I'm movin' out of that old moneysink. Gettin' rid of everything that George, His Majesty the Useless, left me with. All those old messes to clean up, I never even go over there."

Irma gulped, and the memory of wooden floors with bright sunlit windows overwhelmed her.

"Well if you're moving," she said even without thinking, "Maybe I could help clear out some of the old stuff for you. You know, I do a lot of, " she trailed off, "community service and used to volunteer at Goodwill." She had started lying without knowing it. Clearly one of Melissa's more apt traits was bluffing.

"Would you do that? What a dear." Jan shrugged it off, "I was just going to leave most of it in there or let someone do a yard sale."

"Well I'd be happy to help," she said, a bit too enthusiastically, "but I forgot where the house is after all, I don't think I ever visited."

74

Jan adjusted the grip on her grocery bags, "On Walton Street, the furthest street from the main road on Tucket. You just keep making right turns. Number forty. I haven't been there in a while, but the key is under the planter. You should feed the dog while you're there, too. She'll be happy to have company. Know anyone who wants a dog?"

Melissa nearly retched.

"I think I might know someone," Irma replied. "When should I drop by? I have this weekend open. I'd love to make quick work of it." Was the weekend open? It didn't matter. Nothing did. She had to see this place again.

"Yeah that's fine," Jan said with a noncommittal shrug, "I'm off to go please the old man. Good to see you uhhh..."

"Irma."

"Irma. Here, you might want to take this," Jan handed over the bag full of cat food. "They just keep breeding, hard to keep up anymore. See if there's any of those you want either."

Then Mrs. Martin left without much of a backward glance.

Walton Street, furthest from Tucket. She could visualize how to get there, every street, but she'd never driven it before. This will be new, and strange... and different.

As Irma pulled her car into the driveway nearing eleven p.m., she decided to go the next day.

Melissa woke up early and her stomach was sick, she didn't want to have any food but she forced down some breakfast. Remembering her mother's penchant for ignoring family duties, she packed up some snacks for the day and some extra clothes in case she needed to clean. She took what she could and left the house early, visiting her past, with an empty duffel bag under one arm and a fully charged camera.

As soon as Melissa approached the limits of the little mountain town, she navigated by instinct and memory alone, looking at the thirsty brown trees along the road, blending into the warm brown dirt that made up most of the scenery on sloping rock walls. Her little car took the turns well, and she nearly considered it fun since Melissa had never been old enough to drive those roads before. The slow rise and descent of the roads led to smaller canyons lined with beautiful adobe houses for rich folk who "just wanted to get away from it all," and longer roads for people who could afford more land at the expense of good roofing tiles, then down to the houses for vacationers who liked having a hill view of the bigger city below but couldn't stand to visit more than every three months.

That was Walton Street, and she made the last right turn all the way down, thinking she couldn't remember the house number, and realizing she knew all along. The very end of the road, there it was.

The circular driveway looked shorter than she remembered, and the tree in the middle was suspiciously charred, as though it was licked by wildfire flames but miraculously escaped destruction. She pulled around, taking a moment to turn down her stereo before getting out of the car. It was quiet out there, but for some sparse bird calls and an early spring breeze. She closed the car door behind her and looked up at the looming house she used to call home, and her knees went weak. It was so much to take in... and yet... it looked so much worse than she had left it.

The gritty loose asphalt crunched underfoot as Melissa walked toward the sloping porch, thirsty for a coat of weather guard paint that it may never get. There was movement out of the corner of her eye and she saw the last bit of a tail disappear into the door of the garage, which was left ajar. Cats? She didn't recall cats. She only remembered the one. Then her eyes traced back along the porch leading to the front door... and she paused to take it in.

There was furniture everywhere on the deck, but it seemed all wrong. Excess lawn chairs and part of a bistro set were sitting next to full recliners that had no business being out in the weather like that, covered by a porch roof or not. They were out of place and cluttered, one or two holding items like a bucket full of some kind of rope, and a painting. An oil painting of a vase of flowers. What was it? What was its origin and what in god's name was it doing outside? Next to it was a large plastic bowl of water, mostly evaporated and turned yellow, with a few gnats inside. Perhaps it was for the cats. Poor way of treating them. The planter held wizened flowers with a crack up the side that spilled soil in a pool, but she wrestled with the brittle ceramic and found the house key underneath, as promised.

Melissa fiddled with the latch until the large door, the wood and crystal door that once promised the advent of a new and beautiful life for her family, swung open before her.

It was definitely the same house. and the entryway reeked of mustiness and dog urine. It was bright and too warm, the windows doing their duty and reaching sky high to turn the place into a greenhouse. The main floor of the house was large and open, tall ceilinged and lovely. The entry area, she noticed, was cluttered too, an umbrella stand beside the door filled with canes, umbrellas, oddly shaped branches and sticks that Melissa didn't recall ever having or anyone in the family needing, not for any naturalist walking purposes as they suggested. There was another bistro set, decorated up to be a quaint little sitting spot beneath a tranquil painting of boats... which was only a few feet away from another table set, with a different theme, inviting and cute like you'd find in a cafe... and a few feet away... one more, with a vase of fake flowers and a small half-ruined rug underneath, stringy side hidden away towards the wall.

There was a charm to it. Someone had tried to make the hallway pleasant, but it seemed desperate. Stranger still, Melissa knew these half-broken, abandoned table sets were not in the house when she was last there. The paintings had not been around either. Her attention turned to the rest of the house, apprehensive to what she would see, until she heard a scuffle.

There was Flora, wagging her tail in the least bit, and Melissa fell to the ground and cried. She didn't dare take any steps further, and neither did Flora, because she was having so much trouble walking. This precious little dog, no more than forty pounds and sprightly when last seen, was now so large her legs could hardly support her own mass. Her forelegs bowed out, creating ripples in her back as her legs tried to steady a body that had grown so wide. She tried to walk with her back legs completely flat, gingerly and arthritic. The sound of crying made Flora stop short, her tail stopped wagging, and she sniffed the air, confused. The tail wagging started up again, because Flora knew Melissa was back, somehow she could sense it.

Her snout was worn and most of the fur had been rubbed off, pock marked with mosquito bites that she was no longer agile enough to fend off. Her ivory white fur was yellowed, patchy, oily. Her tail was wagging. And she was so glad to see Melissa.

Melissa could not stand to see this happen to something she loved so much.

They hugged for a while, Flora laying down on flanks marked with sores from all the time spent lying down, and Melissa buried her face into her neck and cried, the neck with too much skin for the entirety of her head. Things had gone wrong here. Melissa suddenly knew why she had come back, in that moment she understood. Her sense of responsibility for the family, the house, for everything around her was so great that her soul escaped to continue providing for it.

And this is what she had come back to.

It was proof that being right about the wrong things is one of the worst feelings in the world.

She laid there, quietly taking it in. The dog was thrilled to have a companion, her loneliness was apparent.

Melissa remembered the house the night they moved in, her new bed with the flannel sheets and the feeling that home finally existed. She had slept well, and woke to decorate for Christmas with the rest of her family, placing snow globes on the table and lights on the porch. They had built the house themselves, it wasn't perfectly to their specifications but it stood for a united family, the sheer spirit of them manifested in the walls.

She remembered sitting with her father one night in this new house that still smelled like fresh wood. They sat under rafters that had not yet been lacquered, ceiling lights shining down onto unpainted white walls, uncarpeted construction-wood floors covered by sparse rugs, some mismatched furniture from their old house.

They had talked about school, about her fears in starting high school. He had reassured her, you're going to be great. You'll love high school, he'd said, and whatever you do, we're going to be so proud of you. We already are.

They'd talked about the house, the painstaking detail of making a home custom built for them. He had plans for this house. Those countertops will be granite, flecked with that coral color your mother loves, and we're going to finish up the window sills so that they can have their own indoor herb garden. He always loved to cook.

78

This was going to be home, the place she revisited on Thanksgiving when she had her own family someday, this beautiful house stood for a collective future. I will always provide for you and for this family, he promised her that night, with the dimmed lights and the smell of fresh pine in her head.

Melissa looked around now. The floor still lacked carpet and had substantial water damage, though she could not pinpoint the source. The wood rafters had warped, and ceiling was a graveyard of burnt-out light bulbs looking down upon cluttered, hand-me-down furniture that hardly fit inside the room.

The windowsills were abandoned, the kitchen counters unfinished. Nothing had changed since that day, three years ago. It had only decayed.

When she was fifteen, Melissa's goals were different. She just needed to graduate, and make sure everything was okay for her and Flora, who hated it when people yelled. Flora should have been named Serendipity, because the little abandoned dog had brought so much love into Melissa's life and gave her reason to fight to keep her turbulent family intact.

Little Flora who now laid next to Melissa and wagged her tail even though the hair had been worn away from it, from all the contact with the rough wooden floors.

Everywhere she turned, Melissa uncovered a new memory, and new disappointment. The panic was building in her with everything she spotted, from the ruined kitchen that was overrun by vermin, to her parent's old bedroom that was stacked so high with clothing, furniture and bric-a-brac that she could barely recognize it.

The clutter tried to be cute. Each corner was stashed with a different sign that said "welcome home" or tried to hold your keys for you, coarse wooden placards held by dressed up plush bears with raffia bows. Snowmen, so many snowmen, so many jars on counter tops that might have once held a candle or maybe had no purpose at all. From the towering pile on her mother's bed, she pulled off an old red purse, and a memory along with it.

It was the purse her mother always used, a stylish thing of red leather or some substitute material that always smelled of spearmint, her favorite gum flavor. Melissa always saw it filled to bursting, whether with scraps of paper and miswritten checks or the newest thing Mom brought home with her.

Mom loved buying things. It was how she showed affection, Melissa surmised, with a magpie-like interest in collecting things no matter the price or the purpose. Maybe it made her feel good. Melissa was always accepting little gifts her mother gave her, and rolling her eyes when she brought home a new chair that someone up the street didn't want, or found an antique measuring cup in her favorite color of coral.

The house now showed how that quirk could go if unchecked. Stacks of books (her mom never read anything), end tables missing a leg, clothing that didn't look like it could ever fit any of them... everywhere she turned, Melissa saw new things, collections of objects with no purpose that had crawled their way into their house and stayed quietly broken. Maybe they had a purpose once. Now, they just made it hard to walk anywhere.

This happened because they missed you, Irma said to herself.

No, this happened because without me, they'd have done it anyway, Melissa knew.

Melissa was steeling herself against the hardest step, down the hallway to her room. The smell of dust could not mask the familiar fresh scent of her old living space, somehow keeping its sweetness throughout years of disuse. She paused at the door, stepped into the life she had years ago, and froze as she remembered it all.

The room was *exactly* the same.

The day she died, Melissa was going to a movie night with her friends after school. The girls on the soccer team had little cliques and sometimes got together after practice to do what girls did, eat popcorn and watch movies and gossip about guys. Melissa had trouble deciding which skirt she wanted to wear that day, and went through four of them which she left in a pile on her dressing table, next to the bottle of perfume she always wore. She didn't have time to put the cap back on it that morning, because she was late.

It was all there. Dusty, untouched, just like the last time she saw it.

Gingerly, she reached out and picked up the perfume bottle, smelling it and letting the memories wash over her.

80

Melissa was sucked into this past with memory she uncovered, time passed slowly as she reminisced with every opened drawer, every cracked yearbook. The room was steeped with experiences, every step a different nuance of a life she lived and relived in that moment. Picture albums of kid things and big smiles, inexpert makeup parties and friends she remembered. She wondered if they cried, as she flipped the pages. She wondered why her parents never even opened the door down here. Melissa stared into the mirror she used to look at every day, only to see a pale Irma staring back.

How had she forgotten all this?

The albums she put into her duffle bag, along with her great grandma's cross-stitched pillow and a few tiny things here and there. Nothing of consequence. She could have taken the whole room with her, picked through her old possessions for weeks, but it was too much. She would look in that mirror again, each time the strange reflection looking more pale, more empty. It just wasn't right. She dried her tears, gathered a few important things within reach, and stepped out of the room feeling lightheaded. Flora wagged her tail from her spot in the living room.

Melissa looked out the window just in time to see a tiny creature running away.

She had to visit the garage. ...She had to feed the cats.

The plural of this was worrying her.

The garage was meant for many vehicles, it was enormous inside to account for Dad's latent hobby of building cars. He meant to get back into that, but any space that big must also have been partially storage after a time, though... nothing like this.

It was a maze, a fort of boxes, a dystopian kingdom of abandoned wares. Rolls of old carpeting that never had a home, singular ski poles, boxes of cheap paperback books not worth reading even in their heyday, cracked aquariums with crusty pumps, a plastic kiddie pool tossed into a corner, futons missing backs and couches sitting at broken angles, stacked ten feet high. It looked like a landfill, stretching fifty feet from corner to corner, an unnavigable miasma of hoarded junk. There were no cars in sight, and there never had been.

She heard rustling noises and movement, and saw a cat peering at her from a perch of abandoned chairs. It was an adult cat, but not the same one they had when Melissa was alive.

There was a sour animal smell, as though more than just cats had taken up residence there.

It was a nightmare. Flora wasn't the only creature who suffered this neglect, Mom had created a hostel for feral cats, on the ruins of a family dream.

Melissa was already on her phone, calling animal control to give these animals a home.

She found a dusty plate with remnants of gravy stuck to it, and opened the cans of cat food one by one. One cat emerged from a box on the end

She had their attention. Melissa counted ten of them, as a single tear slid down her cheek.

Only one kitten was brave or hungry enough to approach, leaping at the plate voraciously, a tiny little grey thing that made her heart melt. Without thinking, she grabbed it in one hand, the mewling creature scratching for its freedom, and happened to find a nearby pet carrier in the rubble.

"I'm sorry, I'm so sorry," she said as she imprisoned the tiny creature in a plastic cell, adding a little bit of food so it could still eat. She couldn't stand to watch them all disappear to animal shelters, one of them had to be saved.

The other cats had disappeared, frightened by the kitten's screeching. It couldn't be helped. Melissa took the carrier and closed the door of the garage. She couldn't stand to be there anymore. It was too much.

She didn't want to be Melissa anymore. She wanted to turn off that part of her brain and be Irma again.

She gave Flora a bath, and they laid together on the floor, as Melissa counted down the minutes until six o'clock. At 6:01, she ushered Flora out the front door. Without any guidance, Flora walked straight to the car and stood at the passenger door, looking expectantly at her owner. Melissa started to cry, seeing how eager Flora was to escape this place, trusting Melissa to rescue her like she had done so many years ago. She picked up the cat carrier and placed it in the back seat, the little captive not making a sound. It was time to go.

It was a long drive along old, familiar roads, and Flora laid down in the passenger seat, edging over the parking brake between them to lay her head against Melissa's stomach. She tried to sing along with the songs, and sing to her precious little girl, but her throat was swollen with sorrow. They were happy songs. They spoke of soul mates.

When they arrived, Flora realized wherever she was going, it was not to a new home. Wheedling and treats did nothing, so Melissa did her best to carry the abused animal in through the doors of the veterinary clinic, horrified that others could see them and she would not have the chance to say, this isn't my fault. This creature was left without love. I'd do anything to fix it.

But it was her fault for leaving.

The look on her face said it all as she entered the doors. The receptionist's sugary voice asked, "Is this Flora?" and nods would suffice.

The room was quiet, and for a moment they were alone, Flora staring into Melissa's eyes with a seriousness that said she knew something was wrong. Her neck smelled like shampoo as Melissa buried her face into it, and rubbed her thick, perky ears.

She didn't know if it would work. But it was all she could hope to do.... she went to the car and took out the pet carrier, placing it on a chair close to the table where Flora lay. She made sure the animals could see each other, a ruined dog and a captured kitten, neither certain of why they were there.

Go on.

Go.

It worked for me, somehow, it could for you too.

Melissa looked in Flora's eyes, and wished.

And the doctors showed up.

And they claimed she could take her time.

But Melissa did not linger.

She walked in with a dog, and she walked out without one.

Melissa paid on a meager college budget, and she paid away her shame in failing a creature whom she had promised to keep safe.

The drive back to Irma's house was lonely, just her and the tiny kitten huddled in the corner of the carrier. She sang those happy songs. And she replayed the one about soul mates.

As she pulled into the driveway, she let out a long breath. She didn't leave the car for a long time, just stared at the steering wheel and tried to let go of the feelings, of the memories. She had stood in the middle of a ruined world, lives that crumbled in her absence.

Melissa brought the terrified kitten out of the carrier and perched it on her lap, looking for a sign of recognition. Her thoughts wandered, and she spoke to herself. I will find a way to clean myself of the past, scour the residue of my family rot. I will destroy evidence of the life we lived and squandered together. I will pen my own eulogy, daily, with every memory that emerges and is buried. I will close the book on my guilt with every day I spend with my kitten. I will work to erase even the memory of that life from myself in hopes of letting the new self blossom.

Melissa felt sorry for Irma, for all she had unwittingly become a part of. She hung her head, and wondered how to let it all go.

XI.

Mason

Dearest Mason,

I hope this letter finds you well. Souls come and go, flourish and wither, but from experience they keep moving onwards. We too moved on and though I am not sorry, nor am I convinced you are either, I find myself thinking of you often. Separate ways are not always bad or ill for a relationship. After so long, perhaps we have both changed or stayed the same. I intend to find out.

You would be the best judge of this, as you always were. Your attention to detail and knack for character discovery made you sharp and clever, and I do hope that you find yourself among the brightest of your kind, as you always made possible. I myself? Good health, mentally for the most part, and always an eye on change. We keep our secrets close to our hearts, and begin anew when the time comes.

I'm currently studying astronomy in Los Angeles, the land of smog does not normally seem like a wise place to get a closer look at the sky, but it has been a wealth of knowledge untapped to me. I don't know why I never saw the stars until now; they are so constant and ageless as we ourselves can be. I think sometimes that we are but stars, earthbound and constant like the rest. They say that stars are dead. ....I could probably call this true.

I watch the sky and see the shapes travel, every night. I watch the clouds paint the sky, obscure and steal the attention, and most of all I think that might be where we belong. Amongst the others like Cassiopoeia, Orion and the crux. From our grounded spot, we can watch them above us, and perhaps that was one of our invisible options that we did not know to pick. Do you ever wonder the theory of our existence? The sky is good for that. It seems more tangible to me than it does for others, they believe it seems infinite and humbling. I see it as, someday, possible. I dream. I wonder as I stare up there, I wonder what those stars mean and what they might mean to me. Could it be different? Are they meant to weave a tale to those of us who are patient enough to hear it?

Where would we be if we did not end up here? By now we are studied in our arts, enriching and trading lives, skilled and comfortable at a practiced trickiness of living. I do not wonder why we go on nor what our purpose is, for that is too grand a question to tackle even in the hundreds of lifetimes, but I do wonder how, and if there were other options we did not take.

I regret not a second, not even the time I spent without you. I hear talk of soul mates and I, being in a position to be moderately knowledgeable about some things, do not believe it. But that does not mean that souls were not made to fit together... after all, it is what we do best. We spend lives with others and even when the world said no more, we carried on. But do I believe we do it for one person alone? I cannot, because our time together was grand, but also grand was our time apart. I have done much, lived tenfold and seen more people whom I mistake for others, all so often. We are lucky to have retained ourselves, because most of all I fear that some become recycled... Tell me it has happened to you, where you mistake a name or an instance with another, only to realize you are not who you once were, and neither is this person. It adds a stark realization of how much time has passed, from the days when language was hardly the same and we spoke of different matters in a different tongue.

We traded letters, when we could.

What else have I done? I've sailed a bit, nothing extraordinary. My skill with language has taken me far, and I have had careers both prestigious and banal, whatever suited me at the time. It was on the ocean when I began my love affair with the skies and progressed to being on land, studying while stationary. Before that, I grew to think of history and spent years researching what happened that I never saw when I lived it. There is so much information in the world for us to have and impossible to capture it all in a hundred lifetimes. The stars

86

are much easier to follow. People, however, are happening all the time, and you never know what will be important until it is written in a book that you never knew existed. The world, from every different perspective. I have traveled to historians, spoken with experts, and gathered periods that I may have missed, yet I realized it only made me miss the present. There are so many options afforded to us, Mason. How are we to pick one and be aware of it all?

We cannot.

I have never quested for greatness, or to understand. I believe I have gone on as I have to experience, to see things. There is too much happening in the world for me not to stay an observer, ever entranced with everything there is to see and how it continues, just as I do. Does anything ever really die if the memory remains? I cannot intend to figure it out. I only hope to see what different proof there is, all along the way. Decisions are for lifetimes later, with the possibility of being proven wrong forever afterward.

How often are we wrong, Mason?

I learned languages that grew, changed, and were committed to the vast expanses of memory. I spoke them to gain insight on lives I could never be a part of, and their tales blended together in a Flemish rub of color and the spice of life. I can speak naught of a serenity about me, for after years I am still a person like any other and vulnerable to the moods of any other. We see the daily traffic, the rainy days, the hurt world and its people, and though we above others might be able to help fix it, I personally understand my inability to do so. It is never the act of an individual; it is the job of a shepherd. I am no shepherd. I am...

Perhaps I'm still figuring that out.

What have I done? To affect the world? I listened. Sometimes, an ear is all it might need. I have absorbed without transcribing, experienced without expressing, and enjoyed without much contribution. I think that is a contribution in itself. All the world's a stage, perhaps? If you remember that silly statement? Then that theatre needs an audience. I applaud with gusto, I sense and feel, and I catch a little knowledge along the way. At this rate, with this hope, I may last. I hear woes and discoveries, see art and landscape, I sense the people among us who are as we are. Do you reach out to them? I rarely do. They have their own purpose. I cannot assume it is as broad as mine.

I do think of you, think of "us" as we were and what we experienced. Perhaps due to length and consistency of company, and perhaps that we suited one another for so long. You are also the type that does not share my aims, but that was always why we worked. I've been peering around to catch you again in this life or next. Tracking you down was far from simple. Was it by chance that you are Mason yet again? I have changed so much. I may not be looking hard enough, for even in this world of rampant information I still respect your privacy and the time it takes to tell someone personally instead of saving effort, but I admit I don't know much of your exploits any longer. Old or new. What brings you back to Europe? What grand change do you have in store for all you encounter out there?

The world of questions, from a simple listener as myself. I feel no symphony is beyond you, no novel enough to contain what you bring, so for that I am glad that I do not attempt these things. Leave it to the creators. And I? A hopeful appreciator. A warm mind waiting for the long-delayed update of your life. I will wait for the symphony and the novels which surely will occur someday. You know the types that can. You will inspire them.

I will stare at the stars.

You should look too. We are under the same sky. We might look at the exact same star, and share that connection under the vastness of space as though side by side, wherever we are.

Gazing,
Ethan

88

XII.

Walker

Stories and legends were traded a lot in this small town. It had its share of history and who did what for why and where, including the dastardly tale of how Kirby got his chickens. It was a small, green place, never really exceeded the limit of the small green lifestyle that came with it. They had even upgraded to a real grocery store, though that didn't outclass the general goods market that had been there since the whole town was founded. Just another sort of farmland that nobody paid attention to, but the people in it. From the re-telling, the stories got richer and more distilled until anything was fact and hearsay grew to adulthood. Kirby wasn't even alive anymore, but the memory of his chickens lived on.

There was always an element of fact to these stories, the root which might have been dead on but changed, or added to. There was one story in particular which nobody quite believed but everyone feared, and without the knowledge of the locals, it was actually the one closest to being what it really was. Details were added to scare the kiddies and make sure the teens don't go drivin' too late, and maybe a bit for the adults as well because, well, what the hell happened?

"Nobody knows who she is," they would gather around and say, the kids sitting closer and rapt with the mystery unfolding before them, "But you can see her sometimes..."

Deep stretches of nothing but fields on either side, with just enough grassy wetness between the road and the manicured expanse of crops that a tree might grow, or a pond may exist, or you'd have to want to really get some of that under-ripe corn to pull off to the side and go walkin' for it. They're wet and green and full of clover, no sidewalks in sight 'cause if you're walkin' then the luck is down on you and you might as well just own it, saddle up and sing a song about it later. It was a nice place to be, but you better know where you were goin', 'cause it'd be real far 'til you hit another road and a few more until there was a sign saying anything at all.

These fields were perfect for some of the kids who wanted to borrow the car and get romantic on some random road, for there was no lookout point, just privacy among the lima bean crops that don't tell your mama who you were in the car with. Late at night, not many headlights graced the road, but a fair few had traveled by late from poker night at Johnny's or a teary night among sisters of the township where a little wine was drank. The moon shone down makin' head-lights nearly useless sometimes, but to scare off the wildlife.

It happened some-odd years ago, maybe in the 60's. There wasn't even nothin' hurtful about the story, just spooky, and the people who spoke of it had no reason to tell it other than being concerned citizens and a little out of their wits. Because nobody heard of a disappearin' girl, they knew 'em all.

Then who was this?

She was told to be walking alongside the road, dressed not so kindly but not noticeably wrong, and certainly one of the only moving things on the road late at night,, always after midnight it happened. It was a fact that nobody should be on that road anyway and they reap what they sow, but such a sight was never the pleasantest, a lonesome girl on the road alone, walking. Most just passed her by, as she wasn't in any harm and they didn't recognize her build as a neighbor, and there were folk who stuck to that sort of thing, community is for community only.

Sometimes though, they stopped.

Barney had quite the story he didn't like tellin', of seein' a late teen girl walkin' real slow and cruisin' to the side to see if she weren't hurt. The night was real quiet and he felt like bein' a helpful sort after all the money he'd won on blackjack, which probably shoulda stayed with the Widow Josephine anyway but he'd won it anyhow. He eased his truck to the side, off into the grassy areas a few yards ahead of this gal and automatically reached for his handy flashlight in case some-

90

thin' needed lookin' at. Out of the car door he went, leavin' it ajar and callin' out to 'er, seein' if everything was all right. She didn't do much movin', nor did she acknowledge him at all. She musta looked right through him, as he called out one more time and walked a little bit closer before thinkin' that somethin' was wrong, but it weren't an injury.

Her steps were a burdened shuffle, with seconds of pause in between as the feet slowly found their place and held their weight. Her arms didn't move. She just walked, and her steps were wet against the grass and the clover, making whisper noises as she brushed 'em.

Ffffffum.

Ffffffim.

Barney didn't have a clue what to do. He switched on that flashlight and hazarded liftin it to her, and the light flashed on her face for no more than a moment before he was back in the car drivin' to where things made sense.

When asked what he saw, he shrugged and brusquely answered, "She wairn't no livin' thing."

It was always after midnight, and never quite in the same place along the long stretches of road, and never the same description of who she was or looked like. For anyone familiar with the story, they stopped bein' curious. They see a figure walkin' and they let her walk, and forget they saw her at all. Sometimes the window would be rolled down and maybe they'd hear a bit of cryin'. Maybe it was their imagination after all. She showed up by the willow tree on Hapshead road once or twice, or at least that was one of the only landmarks anyplace to compare to.

A few unlucky and curious folk had slowed over the years, to get a better look and satiate their desire for validity. Trick of the eyes it may have been, but she wasn't no pretty sight. Her body wasn't made to move any longer. Some parts were pale and missin'. The angles weren't quite right. They'd learn not to slow down any longer.

There was some deep speculation, even with some extra details filled in, and this stood out as one of the only stories where there wasn't a definite fact to tell. Maybe Barney had a few nips off the bottle at Blackjack, or had fallen asleep as he drove, and maybe the excited, atrophied imaginations of the late night drivers in the town imagined their own parts of that story, but on whole most of the people faced with it didn't do investigating on any roadside, and were happy to leave well enough alone. It gave them the chills to pass by the occasional pale figure, but they nodded and just said, well, it could be somethin' worse.

Elma never liked the story, she'd get awful quiet and look a bit sad, as though maybe she was sympathizin' with the possible griefs of this girl. Her elderly fingers would stop their recreational stitchin' and she'd wait until the story was through. "The soul knows when it's goin' a leave," she whispered to herself, eyes facing her quilting, "and that one refused to go anywhere."

Well. That'd explain the shamble, then. Just a lonely girl whose body quit before her will did.

XIII.

Carson

SHE WAS FIFTEEN AND SHE WAS VERY BEAUTIFUL. CARSON SIGHED AS he looked at the picture of his daughter on the wall, acknowledging that he was getting older, but that his life kept getting lovelier. His wife, though approaching her mid-forties, looked as beautiful and refined as she ever did, her arms clasped around the neck of her daughter in this picture. They could have been models, sun shining down on glowing blonde hair, laughing faces as they hugged close. All the pictures were like that. He smiled. He was amazed he could be a part of it.

Carson was handsome himself, slightly older than his wife but more susceptible to aging. His hair was already going white around the ears; the wrinkles making his square face seem accomplished. While he was certainly not model material like the pictures he looked at onhf his wall, he made age look respectable and nobody could say he wasn't deserving of the family he had. After all, he was a decently successful businessman, so he must have caught Martha's attention somehow.

Today will be a good day, he thought to himself as he looked at his picture frames in the hallway, adjusting his tie before he left. Everyone was out of the house earlier than him, Mary left for school when it was almost still dark outside--for reasons nobody in the district quite understood, as it inconvenienced families and cantankerous teenagers alike-- and Martha, a pinnacle of self-control and all that embodies the Modern Woman, either did errands or went to the gym after dropping off her daughter. She always liked to drive the sporty little vehicle, and in truth Carson liked to see her in it. Nothing quite like a knockout blonde in a tiny convertible, especially if that woman is his wife. He preferred she drive the SUV to do the errands-- trunk space is naturally limited-- but Mary would jump in and beg him to let them drive the smaller one. He supposed it quelled some of the embarrassment of being dropped off at school by your mother, if she's driving a slick convertible.

His parking space at work was too small for the SUV, but as he looked at the key ring holder by the door, he recognized that once more, they had taken the sports car for themselves. He smirked.

Carson would sometimes wake up early to see them in the mornings. Though Mary slept later than time allowed, Martha would make some breakfast for him, or in its absence, prepare a cup of coffee just the way he liked it. She wasn't always the most demonstrative wife, too serious for him sometimes, but she showed her love in her own ways, primarily through supporting the family. Her small smiles made him melt, the way she would run her fingers through his bed-flattened hair and slide down his arm every morning, to say hello and goodbye as she grabbed the keys and waited for Mary. It was the little things like that. She supported the whole family, filled in the cracks of their being and offered nothing too much. She had her space.

He often wondered if she had ever cheated on him and found another. Then he realized she had no time for it. His paranoia was due to his incredible luck, for he loved her and wondered how he could ever live so close to perfection.

Martha was warm and quiet, reserved, as though she was a benevolent queen with much responsibility and you felt blessed for having her time. Despite looking so much like her mother, Mary was not that sort of girl at all. Carson had given most of his personality to her; she was a little uppity, feisty and colorful. Bright as sunshine on some days, and bratty as a toddler on others, she did not have the restraint of her mother, but that was what made them their daughter. Mary had quite a few friends and even wanted to try out for cheer squad, but she would laugh so much each time she mentioned it that you couldn't tell whether she truly wanted it or not. Just a teenager being a teenager. They lived pretty well as a family, with the right pairs

94

of trendy jeans and fresh healthy meals a few nights a week, a small but elegant house that stayed clean, sharing group nights watching racy drama shows on the premium cable channels.

So maybe life was a little boring. Hell, he couldn't find a better one yet. They all got by just fine, if lacking the excitement and color that a more hectic life provides.

He fixed his tie, it was fine. He smiled at the frames on the wall, and the pictures smiled back. About to tuck his cell phone into his pocket, he was surprised when it rang in his hand. It wasn't a number he recognized, but he answered anyway, grabbing his coat to step out the door.

"Mister Giles?"

"Speaking."

"This is the Lakefront Hospital. There's been an accident."

It felt like everything stopped.

Should he go pick her up?

Should he?

It would be so hard to face. She would know something was wrong and it was not a good place to tell her. How do you break the news? Maybe she's already been called.

He sat on the doorstep of his house in a daze. The door was open, the keys were in his hand, and he could not move, so he'd just sat down. He wanted to go to the hospital directly, right now, but Martha was dead before the ambulance had even arrived. There's no need to rush anymore. He could take as much time as he needed, because he had the rest of his life to be without her. What's the use in hurrying? It still feels like she's alive. He didn't want to get rid of that feeling right away. He had to make it last for years now.

So he sat, and his phone would occasionally ring, and he would let it, as he sat on the concrete steps wondering if this was real.

The funeral had been expensive, a rush of yellow and white and then it was over, all of it was just gone. It was like he remembered nothing, not even his own family condolences or comfort for his daughter, all he knew was that Martha was no longer there to make him breakfast, or drive his little sports car, or to be there as he rolled over every morning.

That was the worst of it. Waking up alone. Wondering why.

His work went on but he wasn't sure if he did well. He wasn't even sure if he showed up. Things might have gotten done, there and around the house, but he was hardly around to see it. He just felt that emptiness and longing that fills the void when love is punctured by circumstance. The house stayed as it was, and in the back of his mind he knew it should change, just to break him out of the same habits of wondering why the coffee wasn't made, and wondering where Mary was going in the mornings without her mother.

The worst part was, the car was fine. Martha was hit in the crosswalk. It wasn't even the man's fault; he was having a seizure and was now in special care. Remorseful, even, but it didn't help Carson cope. It just made it feel worse to be reminded with the letters and flowers sent to the door. The flowers were yellow and white. They looked like her hair. Carson cried when nobody was looking. Mostly, that was all the time.

The car was dusty in the garage next to his, and he treated it as though it wasn't there. Every day it would grow more quiet and dull with lack of use, and each day he let it set there trying to forget why it wasn't being driven. He didn't touch music, the stereo remained quiet. All the songs would be about her anyway.

It took a few months of haze before he got his own coffee and woke up from this dream. The clothes were still in the closet, and the car was still there, though the house was a little bit dirtier than he remembered, there was a presence of more socks in corners that her discerning eye would pick up. He sat down to watch some of the old TV shows he used to like, only to find that the seasons were over. Mary had been going through school all the while, and was getting nearer to summer break and her sixteenth birthday. They had hardly talked since Martha was gone, or if they had, Carson had forgotten it. She seemed to be doing well enough, was quieter than normal and her eyes seemed to have a softness they didn't before. Maybe it was just the effect of seeing her father's heart break. They both lost someone that day. He had been too enclosed to see how it could have affected them both.

One night from his bedroom doorway, he heard music and a warm voice singing along, and peeked his head out down the stairway

96

into the living room. It sounded just like her, but it was just Mary, cleaning up after her homework for the evening, singing one of her mother's favorite songs.

This became a natural occurrence, in fact, one he both hated and relished, for it bathed him in warmth and comfort of a life he once lived, subconsciously feeling that this was right. It was worst when he didn't recognize the difference, and let it hit his ears like nothing was wrong. He got his best work done that way. Then he slept alone.

The mornings became brighter, the weather warmer to where he no longer needed slippers on the thick tile kitchen floor as he went to prepare a quick breakfast. He woke earlier to say goodbye to Mary as she was picked up for school, and she would smile at him quietly and wave from the door, dark mascara eyes looking at him as though they shared a secret bond of trust. It was good that he was waking up earlier for that. Maybe it's part of what he had been missing all along.

She was growing into a fine young lady, Martha's parents had decided to host a family birthday party for Mary, to take the pressure off Carson--and surely the discomfort away from people who would still see the shadows of Martha everywhere in the house, should they come to visit. It was her sweet sixteen and she wore a shirt of her mother's, it flattered her well and she looked her age and beyond. The family hugged her and tears welled in their eyes as they sought comfort in the closest memory of their lost daughter, and sister. Mary wore it well, already a gentler version of who she once was, as though her smile was quieted in reverence to whom she resembled.

It wasn't too long until school was nearly out for the summer, and under the guidance of a neighboring school friend's mother, Mary got her driver's license almost immediately after her birthday. It came as a surprise to Carson, who had not helped in any form, but he realized he must have had some part in it and merely forgotten to take note. After all, the world went on without his attentions, and he was especially proud that Mary had done so well.

He started his mornings earlier now, padding down to the kitchen to find the toast and bacon waiting for him from a proud young daughter who would be perusing her homework one last time to study up for finals. They would talk only the slightest about school work and how she was doing before she would wash out the skillet, and go to leave, ruffling his hair and tracing her hand down his arm before reaching for the keys to that sporty little thing in the garage.

His workload improved. His attentiveness in meetings was sharper, and he had relevant things to say. He smiled a little throughout the day, and would return home a little later than usual to see the soft lights in the living room and the quiet music on the stereo, accompanied by a mellow voice that sang along with certain lyrics. He would watch TV, catching up with the shows he mostly enjoyed, and wait until the lights were out as a signal for bed.

The bed was still empty. The closet was close to vacant as well.

Summer had officially begun and Carson was watching his coworkers tans get darker as their sleeves got shorter. It had been a long time since he had a vacation but going to the lake didn't seem as appealing this time around, so he let himself stay pasty white and wear the same collared shirts he always did. He landed a project that was challenging and rewarding, which he knew was a gesture of trust and empowerment from his boss, and he threw himself into it with a vigor he had been lacking. More nights were spent away from the TV, but those nights by the computer weren't so bad either. The music would still flow in from the other room, whenever Mary was back from the day's events. She had supposedly secured a summertime job at a fashion store, which kept much the same hours as her school did, so things went on as normal.

The car was sparkling clean again, in the garage next to his when he came in at night. Mary would sometimes be making a simple meal in the kitchen, and Carson would kiss her on the cheek and compliment some new fashion accessory she was wearing, a very sophisticated pairing atop one of Martha's designer tops. Carson grew more proud every day, and looked forward to the mornings when his hair would be ruffled as Mary went to work with that enviable car.

It was a Saturday, and Carson had been out for a walk and was just heading back into the house as a blonde in a convertible caught his eye. What a knockout, he thought, as the car slowed and rolled into his driveway. Shaking his head, he stepped out of the doorway to greet his daughter.

Their nights were quiet together, Mary would sometimes join him to watch TV and they would share a couch comfortably while

98

biting into a few Oreos or talking about the current crime syndicate sure to be overthrown any night now. She would talk about work only a bit, thinking she'd prefer something more serious like an internship instead of a job in retail, but she got to meet nice people and they would sometimes meet up for evenings over wine. This was not distressing to Carson, in some way Mary had proven all at once that she had grown up. The phone would ring and Mary would answer, but the conversations would be short and Mary would not head across town to a party that she had clearly been invited to. The phone calls came slower but more deliberately, but Mary often preferred to relax around the house after her usual trip to the gym in the evenings, sharing an impromptu dessert with her dad into the night.

On occasion a movie commercial would catch their eye, and plans would be made for a midweek outing with dinner at one of their favorite haunts. Mary would outdo herself to impress the wait staff, showing up in a classic dress that would make her absolutely stunning. With her hand on Carson's arm, they'd walk into the restaurant, and laugh as the waiter called them husband and wife. In the candlelight, she would radiate the beauty of her mother, and Carson was so proud as she rested her hand on his and gave that subtle smile.

The movie nights were not often, but always fun to go out and order expensive food, and they truly enjoyed each other's company as she talked about her future and new recipes for dinner, and he talked a little about work and mostly listened to her. She had grown more distant with her current friends and felt that she was moving on in life, and he approved of this and the direction she was headed. She was thinking about college or maybe going straight into the work place, although it would be a while for that yet, she felt that college could be handled easily alongside a desk job of sorts so she could take care of herself.

For sixteen years old, she really was blossoming into a lovely young lady, the sort you see in old movies, and Carson liked being there to listen to her talk and think. Sometimes the TV show would be over but they would stay up late into the night discussing the future they each had, or what book she had been reading off Martha's shelf. She said books were like visiting old friends. She would crawl under his arm on the couch and read, straight backed and pretty, and Carson felt like everything was just right.

They discussed going to the lake once more, but put it off in favor of the habit of comfort in their own home. She would sometimes lie outside in the bright sun, skin shining with tanning oil in her stringy black bikini, and Carson would set outside with his sunglasses on in the shade, listening to smooth jazz trailing outside from the open windows of the house. He'd read through the newspaper on these Sundays, possibly giving a shot to the sudoku puzzle, and admire the day, Mary, and everything around him. She never needed help with putting the tanning lotion on, and he admired her independence as he watched her slowly stroke her hands across her toned legs and shoulders, leaving a gossamer trail behind.

He came home later than usual one day, making sure the last step of work was completed with his oversight, and opened the door to his home to see Mary, her blonde hair freshly brushed and draping about her bare shoulders. She was wearing a casual black dress, one that was tight in all the right places and had draping sleeves that added a slinky allure. It was one of Carson's favorite dresses, on his wife. She had coupled it with some new shoes and a barely there necklace made to twinkle in the light and bring attention to the sculpt of her neck. He smiled and came to her, wrapping his arm around her slim waist, wondering what the occasion was before she kissed him on the cheek and headed to the door, saying her phone would be on.

Outside the door, Carson noticed a different car had pulled up into their driveway, and a sharp dressed man leaned against it with a fistful of flowers at his side.

The door closed.

Carson couldn't sleep very well, rolling over and gazing to his side of the bed, wondering when she would be back. The bed stayed empty, but then... it wasn't her bed, either.

The breakfasts were delivered as normal, with the same lingering goodbye Carson loved every morning, with ruffled hair and the touch down the arm. His coffee tasted bitter that morning, but he quickly forgot and learned to just look forward to the mornings and evenings. The second date didn't see him well, either. Another tight stretched dress which he saw walk out the door, and he tossed and turned until

100

a late hour wondering if she was alright. He heard running water in the hallway bathroom and went to check up on her. She was drying off her face, glowing with a lack of makeup, wearing a thin tank top and light pajama trousers, front speckled with droplets from the sink. Carson just wanted to make sure everything was okay, and wondering how the night went. He said he had been worried, but Mary gave him that warm smile and wrapped her arms around his waist, kissing him on the corner of the mouth. She said she was fine. She said goodnight.

Her neck would sometimes get tense from arranging clothes from work, and she would sit in front of him as he worked his fingers into her shoulders, easing all the tension away, and then lean back against him to lazily watch television together for the remainder of the night. It was the kind of closeness he had missed and needed. Her hair smelled like coconut. He sometimes imagined his pillow smelling the same.

The weekly dates continued, sometimes with someone new, but no introductions were made. Carson mentioned he considered playing the field and maybe getting a date sometime. Mary said nothing.

Mary was just living the teenage life, and it was right to be protective of his daughter. Summer was nearing an end and he wanted to make an effort to see his old friends some more, going to bowling nights were the best way to remedy that. He had lost his knack for the perfect strike, but it was the camaraderie that mattered. His friends laughed that he mentioned his daughter so much, calling him quite the domestic. Then they stopped laughing so much, and bowled in moderate silence, Carson talking all the while about Mary and how lovely she had become.

When admiring her nail polish one night, he noted that she wasn't wearing her wedding ring. But those weren't Martha's hands. Mary was just a girl, but she had changed so much. Then she went out to that new car, leaving behind a scent trail of sweet flowers, with that special smile as she kissed him on the corner of the mouth and went to leave. He pulled his head away. Carson sat alone in the TV room wondering if he should find a way to move out.

One night he woke up, and the bed wasn't empty. She had just had a bad dream, she said, giggling shyly and letting her eyelids droop on the pillow beside his, her hair creating a halo of gold wisps around where she slept. Then she snuggled in close, to feel safer.

There was that smell of coconut, like Martha's favorite conditioner.

Oh.

Martha I missed you.

XIV.

SHE WAS OLD AS STORMS, OLD AS BREATH, OLD AS BELIEF. HER HANDS wizened from youth, use, and prayer, and through her the world spoke its tones. The sage smoke in her left hand billowed secrets, the right hand held rocks that mapped answers onto the dusty ground where they fell. Her eyes were old and yellowed, though her body was new and taut. She was the speaker, the Matron, the host, and the mountaintop was her kingdom.

Matron was kept safe and solitary, and she took what she pleased. New hosts, wives, food as necessary, all was given to her in hushed tones, with a bow. She kept the simple folk safe, kept them close to their ancestors and gods, and she was sought for her wisdom and the knowledge of ages.

...This had never been done before. Alien hands ascended the summit, grasping at scraped dirt and pebbles for the last moment of the journey. The Matron was ready, crossed limb in limb with eyes closed, facing him as he lurched to the ledge where she sat. A wind blew all around them, whipping his words back into his mouth as he called them. Instead, she spoke first.

"Welcome."

"Whom am I speaking with?" he asked, without tact, in clipped pronunciation of words that were not his native.

"We are the History."

"I seek to learn from you, elder Matron, I seek many answers."

The wind held their voices between them. His question gained weight, and he wished he could gather it and restate his thoughts. He adjusted the straps on his pack, considering an early departure.

"You are an Outsider. We are interested in you." Her eyes stayed shut and her voice had the rattle of a hive mind. It hummed from her with too many echoes. He believed it real. *"You speak well, but not perfectly. You seek knowledge at the expense of manners. You have tried."*

In the silence, he realized it was his turn to speak.

"I am nervous, and still learning the ways. I am from Down Below, and in the Beyond, I am not an expert. I seek answers. Not about me, about you."

"You ask much."

"I seek great things. Your greatness has led me to you, in the presence of Eyes of Eons. I offer new world knowledge for ancient wisdom."

"We desire nothing of the sort."

"Then you may wish to help a weary traveler along his path to an enlightened world. I have learned what I could of your people, consider me one of them, and guide me."

Their language was archaic and formal, yet he still strained to make out the procession of words that poured from the woman as she sat. She spoke an old tongue, a rock hewn language of intention and pure feeling. He was trying to remember it all in his mind, and hoped his recorder would pick up anything other than the whistling wind.

Matron's eyes slowly opened, cloudy and yellowed, blank as the eyes of the dead. He tried not to react. He tried to remember every detail.

"We will grant you an audience. We will answer only twice."

"So I can only ask two questions?"

The voice was silent.

He tried to remember his burning questions, the phrases he had practiced into a mirror and under his breath for weeks for what he wanted to ask. He had hoped for so much more, but only two will be answered... he asked the first thing on his mind, and gritted his teeth.

"Please tell me about the earliest times."

He heard the answer on the wind, in the way the air felt, in the way the dust was finer, salty, fresh. He could smell the ocean, he could sense the groan of the tallest trees, the cool silt underfoot as the land was new and untouched. The huts smelled of sap, and the fires burnt black each night, casting a shadow of voices and gratitude deep into the friendly dark. Their tools were bones and stone, wood and bracken, baskets and tar. They led animals by strings, they fenced green sprouts with rocks, they sang each night and shared the day's gathering. As the eldest and wisest of them moved on, the young would look for guidance, and indeed they would find it...

The yellow eyes were unblinking, looking past and through him as he regained himself, atop a plateau, with answers, so many answers flowed through him. He was struck silent. These people had domesticated animals, developed tools and a social construct even before they had settled. The ocean had led them to where they were. These were the answers he knew, and yet was lost for where to express them. This changed everything.

Matron was frozen in position, maybe watching him. He had his other questions, so many. Was that really the beginning? Where were they before that? What language were they chanting?

His second question arrived, crudely, and he begged,

"How do you channel the History?"

Please, let it validate everything he's worked for.

Please, be something worth pursuing, let it be revolutionary.

Let his name appear on documents of science, being the first to unveil proof of what others begged they could find.

Let this finally be the moment.

The wind slowed around them, the Matron closed her eyes, and his ears and senses were empty. No, he thought, no please, I need this, I tracked this down, I worked so hard...

But he was met only with silence. Out loud, he pleaded and asked again, suggesting his own theories to spark an answer, any at all. There was none. For the first time, the Matron stirred, moving with the demeanor of an elder yet occupying the body of youth. She approached him slowly, clouded eyes open, and reached forward to touch him on the shoulder.

The cliff was far above him, and it was still where he stood, the wind had not made its way down the mountainside. He had been up there, he remembered the climb and the meeting, but the details were evaporating from his memory. When he raised his recorder to his ear, all he could hear was the whistling wind.

XV.

Cam

THE BLOOD WAS EVERYWHERE, AND CAM KNEW HE'D HAVE HELL TO PAY after this but the rush of the moment was just too much. It was as though every fiber of hatred was pushing that knife into his throat and by god if Damien didn't deserve it.

Was Cam enjoying it? Enjoying watching this man die in front of him, suffering from wounds himself as their injuries bled together in a slippery pool under them? Damien was still strong, struggling, pushing all he could against the arms that were pinning him to the ground on the wet wooden floor. Cam's knees slipped on the slick floor, edging him out of control for a half second and it looked as though Damien would be free. In a last surge of rage, Cam thrust forward just enough to dig the knife deeper into the wound of Damien's throat, and a gurgling sound of muffled screaming signaled the end. Cam pushed, releasing his own carnal scream that was interrupted as a force knocked him backwards, flat on his back.

Had something gone wrong?

Was this dying?

Is this what it really felt like?

A few minutes passed as one man, hardly breathing, laid across from a man who was not breathing at all. The entire place was red, deep, rich and already coagulating around them, and the room reeked of iron. Cam felt his own body, his arm was badly gashed but probably not fatal, just debilitating. He didn't need to do any more fighting tonight, at least maybe he didn't. He just needed to clean up. From this angle alone he knew what a feat that would be, and he gave thought to running out of the house and getting as far as he could, forever away, possibly going to Canada or Mexico. Which was closest? Did he have enough cash to get anywhere?

He calmed himself. The rash approach was not for him. It's what got him in this mess. Cam had taken a man's life for no other reason than fury, and two wrongs don't make a right. The least he can do is clean up, before anyone knew, leave as little evidence as possible, and quietly make his departure.

Probably to Canada.

Fuck Mexico.

The ceiling looked far away and his body was weak, dizzy from the loss of blood and the strain of fighting for his life. He could barely get onto his knees but luckily the bathroom wasn't large, and cleaning supplies were readily available a mere arms-length away. Bleach. *So much* bleach.

Where to begin? Damien's eyes were glassy and staring as though he was knocked out instead of dead, it made it hard for Cam's mind to understand. Dead bodies don't really seem dead. Even the ugly, twisting rip in his throat looked unreal. What does someone do with a body? Should he leave it?

He should just leave altogether. They will find him. The modern world is too advanced for murderers to go missing. The panic was debilitating on top of the strain, my god he could barely keep conscious, but the last thing he could do was pass out on top of a person he had just killed.

Get a hold of yourself.

We can fix this. Or... we can make it better.

He started filling a bath, the water running both cold and hot into the tub, already a pinkish hue from the blood on Cam's hands that ran under the spigot. Water was a good start. Sponges. Soak it up, squeeze it out, bleach. He'd seen some crime scene shows in his day. He knew that there was a protocol and that would at least slow them down. Cam was by no means a primary suspect, so buying time was all he needed to disappear. Actually maybe Europe sounded nice. Go backpacking. Become a monk. Stop being so fucking dizzy when he needed to concentrate.

108

Monks were like ninjas, right? They'd killed men before. He'd fit right in.

The sponges sloshed their macabre offerings into the tub, wrung out by powerful but shaking hands, sopping up more and more but it just seemed to keep coming, every detail, it was everywhere. Cam could be there for hours with the lifeless body of a man that he didn't know what to do with. Maybe put it in a closet somewhere. They'd have to open the closet, and then they wouldn't know where the scene of the crime was. That wasn't so bad. It might be a good idea. More time. Just a few more days' time. He could get to anywhere, like Eskimo towns by then. Learn to fish. Have a pet seal or something. Do whatever the fuck Eskimos do.

Concentrate.

Remember to breathe.

The body can go in a closet. He can clean up the floor. Just sop up the rest of the blood. Just keep turning that tub more and more red. Just....

Cam fell over, weak and twitchy, his body spasming on the wood floor. Stop it. Don't be such a pussy. This just has to get done. Twitch all you want with the ninjas. After we go to the bank. After we use the Lysol all over this damn floor. There's time for being weak, and it's after you've made it to Canada.

His arm was still bleeding, but only so much. It seemed shallower than it at first looked and he snorted at it, it's nothing. Not enough to scare him anymore. Just keep mopping up the floor. He was actually getting somewhere. The floor was streaky and pink but he was close. He should move the body soon, to get the rest of the blood cleaned up underneath.

Cam got on his knees and leaned over the side of the bath to squeeze out the sponge into the deep tub, when he pitched forward and fell headfirst into the water. He thrashed to get himself out but it was a shock, the water felt the exact same temperature as his body, as though he was being pushed on by heavy air. This tricked him, and he inhaled only to choke on cloudy red water, his eyes open and wondering where the surface was, what direction he was in, why his body wasn't letting him move out of it. His legs thrashed and hit walls and his arms tried to push out

109

of the tub from whatever angle he was in, but it's like he was an infant, his body spasming every which way and not letting him move, breathe, or escape. He writhed, but he had lost all control.

Without thinking he let out a roar, the last of his air escaping to the murk around him and by reflex taking in another breath of lukewarm water, tainted with the blood of a man he had just killed. He needed air. His body was flailing and getting nowhere, flopping him upside down and backwards but not above the surface, wherever the surface might be. He couldn't tell anymore.

He was drowning in a tub two feet deep. He was smothered by the blood of a murdered man.

And things got cloudy in his head.

And the fogginess combined with his body wanting to just give up, and lose consciousness.

And he tried to breathe the thick water that kept him down.

Had something gone wrong?

Is this what it really felt like?

Was this dying?

Yes.

You murderer.

We're dying together.

XVI.

Erin

GRETA WAS TAKING OVER THE DINER'S NIGHT SHIFT, THE BORING AND dreadful night shift, for the third night in a row. She wondered how long it would go on. She felt better than that job and opted for quitting rather than becoming the new Graveyard Gal, because her demeanor was not surly enough to fit the bill. She liked mornings. She liked not having to see them hours before they happened. This whole week made her feel like she was irresponsible and doing something wrong as that sun came up.

Plus, the diner was just empty. After a certain hour, nobody really came in unless they were gruff truckers or the occasional pack of teenagers who weren't really hurting anybody, so curfew wasn't strictly enforced. Around the later hours, maybe four a.m., it was hard to get anyone at all before the morning rush. She brought in a crossword and sudoku, and considered upgrading to a book or iPhone game. Nobody was there to care, except Jose in the kitchen who was probably doing the same thing, if not napping.

Third night in a row.

The door opened to the chill outside and a girl walked in, looking younger than she was. She had a vitality and vigor which was rare for the overnight crowd. Maybe she was on drugs. She approached the counter with a skip.

"Just one for you?" Greta asked.

"Just the one," she said, her mouth breaking into a big smile. She must have been nineteen or so, but had an innocent excitement as though she was nine. Underneath her layers of jackets and blonde braided pigtails she was a slim little thing.

Seating was easy, she could have taken up any five booths she wanted and just spread out, but she took the one nearest to the window and happily accepted a menu as Greta went to get water.

"Know what you want already? I could list off some specials."

She looked evenly at Greta, "I want a two egg pancake plate, but I cannot afford it. So I will get a hot chocolate."

Greta had to smile to herself; the matter of fact demeanor of the girl was infectious. "Well, if you can't pay for it, what can you do?"

"I'm very good at telling stories."

"Would you be willing to put your money where your mouth is?"

"I'd be delighted," again showing that toothy grin, and Greta made a mark on the pad.

"You wanted sausage with that?"

"Yes, please."

"Bacon too?"

"It only came with sausage."

"But do you like bacon?"

"I enjoy it when it's crispy."

"Extra side of crispy bacon. I'll be right back with that cocoa."

The mug looked big in front of her, leaking down the sides as the whipped cream topper oozed into the cocoa and made it sticky. The girl smiled like it was Christmas, and sipped carefully to avoid upsetting the mountain of cream. "What sort would you like to hear about?"

"Which one's your best?"

"It's about me, if that's okay. I've had a long time to work on it."

"That would be fine, but who are you?"

"You are Greta," she said, looking at the name tag, "I am Erin. It's nice to meet you."

"Nice to meet you as well," Greta said as she settled down across the booth. Erin's posture was straight and studious, charged with positivity and respect. "What brings you here alone tonight?"

"We'll get to that, I think." She smiled, "It doesn't start in a fantasy land, nor is it once upon a time, nor does it star anyone more exciting than what you're currently seeing right here. But I think it's a good story because I'm still writing it.

"It was a long time ago, when I had those friends, and it certainly seems like it. I guess back then it was easier to make lasting friendships because you didn't have to worry about technology, or location or anything. There weren't many people around and you were all unofficially family. It was getting towards a point where that was changing, the world was getting bigger, and travel was easier so new groups were mixing. It was exciting! I mean, there you are with your friends who you love through thick and thin, and then there's even more people to know!

"We were really lucky, too, my friends and I; there were only a few of us. We were really close and it was by choice not just location. We loved each other very much and knew that the option was there to cause trouble, and we just didn't. My best friend was Nora, we would constantly make each other laugh and finish each other's sentences. We hardly ever disagreed and she was a little more judgmental and dramatic than I was, but we always felt like soul mates and eventually formed an unofficial pair within the group we had. I was close to everyone, like Felicity and Parker and Jonah, and the five of us were trusting, fun, and didn't always agree but always made it work. We didn't know how lucky we were. Our lives were just that simple and lacked all the hurt that others might have had.

"Then it felt like the borders of where we lived expanded, and travel was less of a barrier. We started to meet new people with their own ways of living, sometimes so different from our own. It was exciting. Weekends were filled with gatherings, with people from nearby places we had never been to. We hardly left our town, people came to us instead. Maybe we were just the easiest place to meet at, the closest to all places, a natural meeting point. My friends and I were considered young, though it was nearly time for us to be making families, and suddenly our age group had so many more people in it, each with their own hierarchy to learn. Am I doing well so far?"

Greta blinked, "Yes, actually, I was quite interested. It sounds nice, having those friends. Will you give me a minute to check on your food?"

"Yes please."

Greta brought back a heaping plate of eggs, pancakes, hash browns and a few extra servings of meat. Erin was all smiles as she seasoned her food politely and took quick dainty bites of her eggs, "Forgive me if I eat quickly and interrupt my story. This is really good and I'd hate for it to go cold."

Greta nodded, "Whenever you're ready."

"With the new visitors, it was like having a party all the time. Their groups were bigger, harder to classify, but some of the notable kids really wanted to be friends with us. It felt like diplomacy sometimes, if we'd known what that was. But we were just teenagers."

Greta stopped to reconsider how old this girl must be if she said she was a teenager a long long time ago, but time and experiences can be relative to those who live them. She stayed quiet.

"There was one girl. Samantha. She was beautiful and I think she knew it, but it was hard to keep track of all the new people in our midst who were all fresh and attractive to our worn eyes. Oddly enough, as soon as I spoke with her, we got along quite amazingly. She took to our group very well, and admitted to me that she had felt out of place in her own town for a long while, since a relationship with her and a boyfriend had ended. It was rare for relationships to end back then, so she had made herself something of a widow and a pariah while her boyfriend stayed as popular as he was. We didn't like hearing the gossip of it, much as she liked to impart it on us, but openly invited her to take part in our group more often if it would make her feel welcome. She was a nice person.

"Somehow it was the way she looked at me... Something about it was special. I couldn't help but be drawn in."

"Over the weekends she became a fixture to our visits and festivities, more than any other person, and diplomacy began to change. With all this increased connection of towns, new loves were blossoming, new friends were emerging and I found myself growing closer to Samantha. Her affection for me was becoming clear, and it was overwhelming. She would pick flowers for her hair and make wreaths

114

for my home. This constant stream of heartfelt gifts was none I was used to, especially not from a lady. It was quite unheard of at the time. It was only a matter of time until we were in love."

Greta nodded a bit, surprised but understanding of how small towns could see that type of love and behavior. This must be the part of the story where things begin to go wrong.

"I hadn't known her that long, so I admit that it was foolish of me. But it is overwhelming to be adored, and easy to fall into. Plus everything seemed so right. She fit with my town, my friends. I thought it would all be right, to openly proclaim that we were courting.

"It wasn't."

Erin paused, fork hesitating over the dregs of her dinner, scraping together the last bites thoughtfully.

"I was seen as a traitor. I never understood or valued what I had been building for myself within my town, and that was a pair with Nora, who felt she had been replaced without her knowledge. It was never my intention, because Nora meant the world to me, she was someone I wanted at my side forever and didn't know that on her end, it meant something very different. I was stupid for not being more aware and respectful of her. She had been preparing to marry me. This was apparent to everyone but me. I would have been the proper husband for her to take."

Greta was yanked from the throes of the story once again to realize that Erin was talking about being a man. Yet the girl in front of her was no man. There was no doubt at all, she was female. Greta could no longer process what she was hearing.

"Samantha and I were crushed. The outcast was once again cast out, and I with her for having made an ignorant choice and hurting others. The word traveled around the surrounding areas, and an even more startling one met my ears: Samantha had been preparing to marry the man from the other town, who was utterly blindsided by our connection. She was no widow as she had said. She admitted it to me in confidence that she had continued with her betrothal until she felt such a strong connection with me, and wished I wouldn't have said anything so openly.

"But I wasn't aware that it was anything to be ashamed of. We stood alone, together, an Abandoner and an Adulteress, all eyes on the

cruelty we had wrought which had been sown from the purity and innocence of love. The factions grew ever tighter with this dual-betrayal,
other men had their eyes on Nora and all were scornful of me and the
one I had chosen above my station and family.

"It was a mistake, a misunderstanding, and Nora and I talked
through it as best we could. The best of friends could not be divided,
but a certain pressure was put upon from all sides, as she was hurt but
also logical. Our interactions were strained but Nora defended me,
understanding my ignorance though not fully accepting it. Of all people, she was the one who stood up for me, the one I had most gravely
wronged, yet pack behavior was what it was and they did not forgive
me for what I had done to her, even if she had.

"It happened so quickly, Samantha and I feeling the strain on
our love and abandoned by all of our worlds. I stood no chance of
redemption where I was, so I was respectful and stood in the shadows, trying to bother no-one, and putting emphasis on my love with
Samantha. If we had ruined ourselves for one another, our love should
stay strong and keep us together in this time of hardship. It better be
worth it. I threw my life into hers, no gift was too much for my be-
loved, nor any gesture too much from her. I worked so hard, we both
did, to keep our last vestiges of self in one another.

"But there was a dark cloud above us, and love cannot fill a void
when all other happiness is lost. We clung to one another, but I knew
I was unhappy. In a short while, it was clear that I was seeing Samantha less, that she was becoming harder to contact. I would find her
love notes left in secret around the house, my eyes would fall on the
little gifts she had placed there, and I would smile and send word of
my thoughts being with her. I received little reply.

"As quickly as it had come, Samantha was gone. Unreachable,
my passionate lover and reason for living. My world had turned
upside down, there were stories of her fleeing back to her town and
under the wing of her once-husband, while Nora and I still were
pained to speak and others thought not of me at all.

"My foolishness had led me to destroy what I had, for love. Now
the reason for the destruction was gone. And I never had the chance
to truly enjoy it.

116

"It seems easy to think of, in retrospect, but I cannot blame myself for the love of another. Samantha had a magnetism that I could never explain, and it was not my love of her that I blame myself for. Foolish it may be, but inevitable with the effort she put into making my life beautiful, and my eagerness in wanting her in that beautiful life. I do kick myself for not understanding who I was in my life, and what it meant, and what I had to lose. I lost it all.

"I did the only thing I could, and perhaps the most cowardly option, is that I left. I would blacken the doorstep of my old friends no longer, I allowed my house to be given away and took to a trail without a destination and without a possibility of return. When you lose it all, they say you have all to gain... but my thought is... that I will live life simply. And I have since."

Erin gestured to the stuffed backpack she had resting next to her, giving it a quick pat. Greta had to look away from the eyes she had been fixed on and see the girl in front of her, the cheery young thing with the love for life, rather than the voice of a boy who had lost things.

Erin was right: she was a very good storyteller. Greta wondered why she wasn't a novelist, with her way to convince the listener of past deeds and lives, but maybe that's what this girl truly is. A bard of her time.

"Did you want a slice of pie or anything, hon?"

Erin considered her empty plate for a moment, deliberating. "Only if you share a few bites with me, Greta."

"It'll be my pleasure. Chocolate silk suit your fancy?"

"If that is your specialty!"

The dim sunrise was edging over the hills, a plate of pie was between the two girls and they smiled as they shared it, Greta noticing that Erin's smile was not only bright, but wise.

"You said the story would come around to how you got here," Greta said.

Erin had her childish voice again, full of wonder, hardly the same voice that spoke of past heartbreak. "That's a lot longer of a tale, really. But the origins are laid out. I never decided to get comfortable, and I was sad at having lost what I loved that I wanted to find new things to love. I found them, along those roads alone where the trees

117

were thick and I loved everything I saw. How the trees grew together as though they supported one another, with ivy snaking between them. With every new person I met, especially those who treated me kindly like yourself.

"The world is full of fleeting things that people try to hold on to, and tuck away in locked chests and keep. But you can't tuck away a sunrise. And I've seen almost all of them. The more we burden ourselves with keeping, the less new experiences we have, for we sit in the same places, and eat with the same heirloom silverware, and never think of what the other chairs might feel like, or the other silverware might sound as it taps against a plate. People like being stuck, it gives them a feeling of building a life, a fortress of memory and comfort where the walls can crack and break so much. I don't want to repair my life, I want to live it.

"I have given up the things I care about so often. I know what it is like to give things up, I know what it is like to lose everything, that I am happy every day I have them. I don't have a home, and I haven't for... well, since back then, since things were different. But I have a perspective, and I have a knowledge of life, and I have the connections I've made with people that last forever in memory. I had a warm meal this morning, I got a new pair of shoes just as the other one was getting old, and I have a smile.

"The world is out there! Every day there's a sun and it shines over lives and people, and things, and if I'm not there to look at the grass and appreciate every grass blade, and if I'm not there to hear the wind rustle the trees near a house and appreciate the sound, and if I'm not around to bring a smile to the faces of others as I remind them that stuff is stuff, and it's only important because of what we make it into, then where would I be?

"I've been a million things, and shared with a million people! I tell stories of fun things that nobody is around to document, and I remind people of different lives out there. Or I try to. I'll trade a tale with a trucker to get a ride to Miami. I'll carve a wand for a kid if he gives me a corn muffin. I'll talk about the beaches in California and the conversations I've heard in Denver. I made the mistake of not valuing others, once. Now, and ever since, it's what I value the most.

"I think it goes both ways. I think people feel better knowing they gave to someone, even if they don't ever get to know me even half as much as you just did, Greta. I think we had enough time to tell most of the bigger story, because a story about husky puppies in Alaska wouldn't have had the same impact on someone like you. I collect these things and share them, and I try to give away experiences. I'll admit, it worked really well in the sixties." Her vibrant grin was back, reflecting in the first beams of sunlight as they pierced through the smeared window.

Greta's voice was rough in the mornings, "Have you thought about going back to your old friends?"

Erin's smile faded a bit.

"Nora's gone. If she wasn't, we'd have found each other by now. I wonder if soul mates really meant what I think it did."

The door creaked and opened as the first patron of the morning entered for breakfast, and Greta excused herself to assist him. When she turned around, Erin was gone from her seat, having left a careful sum of two dollars on the table, a napkin that read "Thank you" in black ink, and a small clothing button shaped like a sun. Greta wondered if she meant it as a reminder of their time and her outlook, but she quickly found a safety pin and stuck it to the front of her work shirt, smiling as she cashed in the bill for one hot cocoa, and a shared story.

XVII.

Anna

It isn't a curse, it couldn't be. But it feels like it is.

The last time I saw your face, it was smudged with blood. It mixed with the grime on my hands as I saw those eyes fade out and fade away.

It took a long time to forget. It wasn't quiet and it wasn't cold. It was warm and rich with the depth of life, vibrant colors from your sweater all the way down to the blood. Anna, I couldn't sleep for weeks. I knew you could be back tomorrow, but it never happens that way. We have to wait. Everyone else thought I was crazy, but in truth you drove me crazier than normal. It was so violent. Sudden is one thing. Knowing what your organs looked like... that's a whole other story.

What is it that you remember?

I couldn't shake that memory, though the funny thing is, to calm myself, I remembered my last moments with you. In the hospital, everything was fuzzy. You glowed in front of me like the angels they always told us about. Do you think that's what we are, angels? I didn't think so either. But to me, you are. You always will be.

It was the most peaceful part of my life. Knowing that you'll always be there. I know it was a long time ago but it feels like yesterday. I remember how you sound when you speak Italian. Your voice loves those words, I don't know how you don't relearn it every time.

I remember Venice. It felt like one, long day. We never slept, did we? All five days or so. It was a photograph of traffic lights... all streaking colors to me. Maybe I had too much of the wine, and too

120

much of you at the same time. The accent really did it for me! You've never been more expressive. Was it the wine's fault again? I loved it anyway, I love you.

Yes I remember what happened after that.

Venice was a random shooting. I remember being scared and holding your hand under the table. Then I didn't even know what tables were. It erases that. You just stop. Don't you?

I mentioned the hospital already. Then there was the stroke. I only saw you afterward. That was early... I wasn't even expecting the phone call. I thought, twice couldn't be a trend, it was unlucky. I think that's the one that really set it for me, the receiver in my hand just listening to it and thinking.... our bodies will even find ways to do it on their own. I already cherished every moment I had with you, but now I know it's down to every minute.

That was dragged out... that was the other car accident. Of course I can't forget that. You had blood on your forehead, every-where, I remember kissing your head and it was sticky and I didn't care. Christ, do you think they keep getting harder? Let's go back to the carbon monoxide days. Holding your hand in bed, not knowing it would be over. I think of that too. Having experienced it, I can say that one was the easiest. We just woke up other people, somewhere else. But our last moments, I was smelling your neck and thinking how lucky I am.

Of course I remember what I was thinking. I couldn't figure out how we died, I recounted that moment so many times until it made sense. And to think, you were only a town away from me those whole three years. Hah, it seems like we have to set up a code or something, darling. But it doesn't matter. Every time I find you, again.

Yes. It was the first thing I noticed about you, other than you staring at me. It's natural to have your eyes drawn to tattoos, it's why people get them. I saw that lovely script and thought, this woman has something to say, something that means a lot to her. I looked at it and... I thought what a lovely way of explaining the situation I'm in. Then, all I remember was your lips, I could tell by touch alone.

It's so beautiful, right there on your collar... "L'Amour, La Mort"... I know, it sounds better when you say it. I'm surprised you didn't use Italian. The... play on words wouldn't work so well, I suppose. Did you know you would find me there? Happenstance as usual. L'Amour La Mort.

Do you believe in fate?

I kind of have to. I don't believe in curses. But I also don't try to make sense of what this is, I'm past it. I'm over it. The world sends you to me, and me to you, and that's what matters.

Anna, do you promise...? Just listen to me, do you promise that next time, we'll say it again? We'll find a way to find each other. No, think about this with me now, so we know. Someday. Some website we can search and find it. ...Why?

The most we've ever had is two months. I want to see if... if we can beat that record.

I suppose it is, I guess we have to trust it. Of course I trust it. I also worry it'll be the last time. Ever. What if this time, you don't come back...? What if I wait for years looking at pretty faces and I never see you. If fate doesn't work for us that time.

I know. It's just that I worry. I've had a lot of time to worry. I love you. As many times as I need to. So.... you don't have to promise. But if you do... maybe something will be there. It's just a new chapter in how we find each other.

Of course I get lonely. But I don't get lonely for companionship, I get lonely for you. It's a very different feeling. We're linked. Nobody would believe me, anyway, that I wait through years to spend five days with you, and have held you in my arms as we've died. Who would believe that?

I've kissed your tears. I like the ones when we meet each other best. They taste like joy and memories, and different every time. The world stops for you.

Are you hungry? What do you want for dinner? We'll order it. Anything, we'll find it. Where do you want to go? We'll buy new clothes so we don't worry about laundry, we'll buy paint and draw ourselves on the walls of our apartment. My love, I don't know how much time we have... it could be anything. Let's do whatever we want.

We discovered your allergy, too late, in Maine. We had two weeks, taking pictures of clouds in Vancouver. You wrote me notes on the mirror every morning in London, and I kept each one, all eight of them. The fire burnt up everything that reminded me of you, and

122

I had to start again. Just with memories. I went under for surgery in Oregon and remember saying, I'll see Anna again.

Every time, your purse is bigger than your torso. And you can't stop singing Christmas songs, even in July. It's how you say things, it's that sound in your voice with certain words that are always there... how you say "envelope" and will always find a way to call out "chicanery." Darling, I've missed you.

I've seen thousands of eyes that aren't as sparkling as yours. And that smile, you can't hide it, no matter what lips they are on. You smell the same, did you know you do? You're sweet and earthy like an orchard. And your fingernails are always long, anything can change but there she is again, with those talons of hers, ready to dig into the world. All of it.

I've lost you, forever, so many times. And I'd do it all again.

XVIII.

The Song Fades

THE SONG PLAYS OUT, INCHES ALONG WALLS AND SKATES ALONG THE currents of air, taking dust particles along with it. It starts slow and passive, but creeps up in intensity, and the listeners don't notice they're listening.

They feel it. It has an urgency. It sings an emotion that has no name, a choice to be made that has no solution, an impending moment that only some have felt. The song calls out, the piano lovely to people who hear, and reminiscent to people who understand.

It waxes and wanes, ebbs and flows; the song carries the memory of pleasure and of disconnection. It approaches that moment with quickened breaths and accompanying strings, it swells across the ears and into the borrowed mind.

It refreshes what is valuable. It cleans away the fogged mind to uncover the deep emptiness when a soul is without a vessel. It palpates rhythms that echo in the space between our decisions and our realities. It reassures and comforts them, as they stand rapt with their mind elsewhere, sharing a moment that only they understand, as the song talks.

It speaks of desire, and dedication. It speaks of not letting go. It speaks of the adventurous unknown, or dissatisfaction, or that the end has come too quickly and a panic sets in.

It's about taking your own destiny, or losing it to chance and trying again. It is about being thrown and ripped from the life you knew, or leaping with open arms with trust in the entire world to catch you.

It is about only one moment, a moment more important than the ones they stay around for. A build up of transition.

It talks about the reasons why, when nobody else can put a finger on it.

Why they had to stay. Why they wanted to. What was left undone. What was finished and needed reclaiming. What was eternal and what was fleeting. Why they said goodbye to all that was familiar and abandoned all natural progression beyond, in favor of doing it all over again.

It felt heavy. Perhaps ugly or perhaps driven with the velocity that outweighed the life it was given. It felt light and inspired, or surprised. When words were not working, someone out there had manifested the moment into music. And it was being heard.

In a friend's car on a tinny radio.

In a bookstore as the dusty volumes absorbed the stray notes.

Alone in a dark room.

They were reliving a moment. They were sharing a kindred memory, burdened with meaning of so many souls who sought not to move on, but to live again.

The song begins, and they remember the moment it all changed.

Then the song fades away, and they wonder if they were right.

 # Thanks.

Most of this book was written for National Novel Writing Month 2010 so foremost I'd like to thank the Office of Letters and Light for pushing me to the limit.

I want to thank Wednesday Wolf, for reading it and reading it again, Benjamin Snyder for giving it a fine-toothed grammatical comb, and early readers like Brad Lawson, Brian Sunter, and Tully Ackland for being creeped out right when I hoped they would.

To anyone who supported me when I talked about it,

To anyone who shared an experience that got me thinking and got me writing,

To Bombay Sapphire Gin for reasons undisclosed but probably to do with long nights of editing,

Thanks millions.

And thank you.
May your soul live on, wonderfully.

About the Author

Nika Harper is a writer, performer, and geeky personality who spends long, solitary nights on the internet because her brain *won't shut up*. She lives in Los Angeles, CA, where she houses her collection of magic wands and an overwhelming stockpile of empty journals.

You can check to see if she got any new tattoos recently at ThisisNika.com, and if you liked the book you can tweet her @NikaHarper.